D1432992

A GEHENNA FACSIMILE

ALCUIN:
A DIALOGUE
CHARLES BROCKDEN BROWN

EDITED WITH AN AFTERWORD
BY LEE R EDWARDS

GROSSMAN PUBLISHERS   MCMLXXI

ALCUIN: A DIALOGUE

PART I

I called last evening on Mrs. Carter. I had no previous acquaintance with her. Her brother is a man of letters, who, nevertheless, finds little leisure from the engagements of a toilsome profession. He scarcely spends an evening at home, yet takes care to invite, specially and generally, to his house, every one who enjoys the reputation of learning and probity. His sister became, on the death of her husband, his house-keeper. She was always at home. The guests who came in search of the man, finding him abroad, lingered a little as politeness enjoined, but soon found something in the features and accents of the lady, that induced them to prolong their stay, for their own sake: nay, without any well-defined expectation of meeting their inviter, they felt themselves disposed to repeat their visit. We must suppose the conversation of the lady not destitute of attractions; but an additional, and, perhaps, the strongest inducement, was the society of other visitants. The house became, at length, a sort of rendezvous of persons of different ages and conditions, but respectable for talents or virtues. A commodious apartment, excellent tea, lemonade, and ice—and wholesome fruits—were added to the pleasures of instructive society: no wonder that Mrs. Carter's *coterie* became the favourite resort of the liberal and ingenious.

These things did not necessarily imply any uncommon merit in the lady. Skill in the superintendence of a tea-table, affability and modesty, promptness to inquire, and docility to listen, were all that were absolutely requisite in the mistress of the ceremonies. Her apartment was nothing, perhaps, but a lyceum open at stated hours, and to particular persons, who enjoyed, gratis, the benefits of rational discourse, and agreeable repasts. Some one was required to serve the guests, direct the menials, and maintain, with suitable vigilance, the empire of cleanliness and order. This office might not be servile, merely because it was voluntary. The influence of an unbribed inclination might constitute the whole difference between her and a waiter at an inn, or the porter of a theatre.

Books are too often insipid. In reading, the senses are inert and sluggish, or they are solicited by foreign objects. To spur up the flagging attention, or check the rapidity of its flights and wildness of its excursions, are often found to be impracticable. It is only on extraordinary occasions that this faculty is at once sober and vigorous, active and obedient. The revolutions of our minds may be watched and noted, but can seldom be explained to the satisfaction of the inquisitive. All that the caprice of nature has left us, is to profit by the casual presence of that which can, by no spell, be summoned or detained.

I hate a lecturer. I find little or no benefit in listening to a man who does not occasionally call upon me for my opinion, and allow me to canvass every step in his argument. I cannot, with any satisfaction, survey a column, how costly soever its materials, and classical its ornaments, when I am convinced that its foundation is sand which the next tide will wash away. I equally dislike formal debate, where each man, however few his ideas, is subjected to the necessity of drawing them out to the length of a speech. A single proof, or question, or hint, may be all that the state of the controversy, or the reflections of the speaker, suggest: but this must be amplified and iterated, till the sense, perhaps, is lost or enfeebled, that he may not fall below the dignity of an orator. Conversation, careless, and unfettered, that is sometimes abrupt and sententious, sometimes fugitive and brilliant, and sometimes copious and declamatory, is a scene for which, without being much accustomed to it, I entertain great affection. It blends, more happily than any other method of instruction, utility and pleasure. No wonder I was desirous of knowing, long before the opportunity was afforded me, how far these valuable purposes were accomplished by the frequenters of Mrs. Carter's lyceum.

In the morning I had met the doctor at the bed-side of a sick friend, who had strength enough to introduce us to each other. At parting I received a special invitation for the evening, and a general one to be in force at all other times. At five o'clock I shut up my little school, and changed an alley in the city—dark, dirty, and narrow, as all alleys are—for the fresh air and smooth footing of the fields. I had not forgotten the doctor and his lyceum. Shall I go (said I to myself), or shall I not? No, said the pride of poverty, and the bashfulness of inexperience. I looked at my unpowdered locks, my worsted stockings, and my pewter buckles. I bethought me of my embarrassed air, and my uncouth gait. I pondered on the superciliousness of wealth and talents, the awfulness of flow-

ing muslin, the mighty task of hitting on a right move-
ment at entrance, and a right posture in sitting, and on
the perplexing mysteries of tea-table decorum: but,
though confused and panic-struck, I was not vanquished.

I had some leisure, particularly in the evening. Could
it be employed more agreeably or usefully? To read, to
write, to meditate; to watch a declining moon, and the
varying firmament, with the emotions of poetry or piety
—with the optics of Dr. Young, or of De la Lande—were
delightful occupations, and all at my command. Eight
hours of the twenty-four were consumed in repeating the
names and scrawling the forms of the alphabet, or in en-
graving on infantile memories that twice three make six;
the rest was employed in supplying an exhausted, rather
than craving, stomach; in sleep, that never knew, nor desired to know, the luxury of down, and the pomp of tis-
sue; in unravelling the mazes of Dr. Waring; or in
amplifying the seducing suppositions of, 'if I were a
king,' or, 'if I were a lover.' Few, indeed, are as happy as
Alcuin. What is requisite to perfect my felicity, but the
blessings of health, which is incompatible with periodi-
cal head-achs, and the visits of rheumatism;—of peace,
which cannot maintain its post against the hum of a
school, the discord of cart-wheels, and the rhetoric of a
notable landlady;—of competence—My trade preserves
me from starving and nakedness, but not from the dis-
comforts of scarcity, or the disgrace of shabbiness. Money,
to give me leisure; and exercise, to give me health; these
are all my lot denies: in all other respects, I am the hap-

piest of mortals. The pleasures of society, indeed, I seldom taste: that is, I have few opportunities of actual intercourse with that part of mankind whose ideas extend beyond the occurrences of the neighbourhood, or the arrangements of their household. Not but that, when I want company, it is always at hand. My solitude is populous, whenever my fancy thinks proper to people it, and with the very beings that best suit my taste. These beings are, perhaps, on account of my slender experience, too uniform, and somewhat grotesque. Like some other dealers in fiction, I find it easier to give new names to my visionary friends, and vary their condition, than to introduce a genuine diversity into their characters. No one can work without materials. My stock is slender. There are times when I feel a moment's regret that I do not enjoy the means of enlarging it.—But this detail, it must be owned, is a little beside the purpose. I merely intended to have repeated my conversation with Mrs. Carter, but have wandered, unawares, into a dissertation on my own character. I shall now return, and mention that I cut short my evening excursion, speeded homeward, and, after japanning anew my shoes, brushing my hat, and equipping my body in its best geer, proceeded to the doctor's house.

I shall not stop to describe the company, or to dwell on those embarrassments and awkwardnesses always incident to an unpolished wight like me. Suffice it to say, that I was in a few minutes respectfully withdrawn into a corner, and fortunately a near neighbour of the lady. To her, after much deliberation and forethought, I addressed myself thus: "Pray, Madam, are you a federalist?"

The theme of discourse was political. The edicts of Carnot, and the commentary of that profound jurist, Peter Porcupine, had furnished ample materials of discussion. This was my hint. The question, to be sure, was strange; especially addressed to a lady: but I could not, by all my study, light upon a better mode of beginning discourse. She did not immediately answer. I resumed—I see my question produces a smile, and a pause.

True (said she). A smile may well be produced by its novelty, and a pause by its difficulty.

Is it so hard to say what your creed is on this subject? Judging from the slight observations of this evening, I should imagine that to you the theme was far from being new.

She answered, that she had been often called upon to listen to discussions of this sort, but did not recollect when her opinion had been asked.

Will you favour me (said I) with your opinion, notwithstanding?

Surely (she replied) you are in jest. What! ask a woman —shallow and inexperienced as all women are known to be, especially with regard to these topics—her opinion on any political question! What in the name of decency have we to do with politics? If you inquire the price of this ribbon, or at what shop I purchased that set of china, I may answer you, though I am not sure you would be wiser for my answer. These things, you know, belong to the women's province. We are surrounded by men and politicians. You must observe that they consider themselves in an element congenial to their sex and station. The daringness of female curiosity is well known; yet it is seldom so adventurous as to attempt to penetrate into the mysteries of government.

It must be owned (said I) there is sufficient reason for this forbearance. Most men have trades; but every woman has a trade. They are universally trained to the use of the needle, and the government of a family. No wonder that they should be most willing to handle topics that are connected with their daily employment, and the arts in which they are proficient.—Merchants may be expected to dwell with most zeal on the prices of the day, and those numerous incidents, domestic and foreign, by which commerce is affected. Lawyers may quote the clauses of a law, or the articles of a treaty, without forgetting their profession, or travelling, as they phrase it, out of the record. Physicians will be most attached to livid carcases and sick beds. Women are most eloquent on a fan or a tea-cup—on the furniture of the nursery, or the qualifications of a chamber-maid. How should it be otherwise? In so doing, the merchant, the lawyer, the physician, and the matron, may all equally be said to stick to their lasts. Doubtless every one's last requires some or much of his attention. The only fault lies in sometimes allowing it wholly to engross the faculties, and often in overlooking considerations that are of the utmost importance to them, even as members of a profession.

Well (said the lady), now you talk reasonably. Your inference is, that women occupy their proper sphere, when they confine themselves to the tea-table and their workbag: but this sphere, whatever you may think, is narrow. They are obliged to wander, at times, in search of variety. Most commonly they digress into scandal; and this has been their eternal reproach; with how much reason perhaps you can tell me.

Most unjustly, as it seems to me. Women profit by their opportunities. They are trained to a particular art. Their minds are, of course, chiefly occupied by images and associations drawn from this art. If this be blameable, it is not more so in them, than in others. It is a circumstance that universally takes place. It is by no means clear, that a change in this respect is either possible or desirable. The arts of women are far from contemptible, whether we consider the skill that is required by them, or, which is a better criterion, their usefulness in society. They are more honourable than many professions allotted to the men; those of soldier and barber for example; on one of which we may justly bestow all the contempt, and on the other all the abhorrence we have to spare. But though we may strive, we can never wholly extinguish, in women, the best principle of human nature, curiosity. We cannot shut them out from all commerce with the world. We may nearly withhold from them all knowledge of the past, because that is chiefly contained in books; and it is possible to interdict them from reading, or, to speak more accurately, withhold from them those incitements to study, which no human beings bring into the world with them, but must owe to external and favourable occurrences. But they must be, in some degree, witnesses of what is passing. There is a limited sphere, in which they are accurate observers. They see, and hear, somewhat of the actions and characters of those around them. These are, of course, remembered; become the topic of reflection; and, when opportunity offers, they delight to produce and compare them. All this is perfectly natural and reasonable. I cannot, for my life, discover any causes of censure in it.

Very well, indeed (cried the lady), I am glad to meet so zealous an advocate. I am ready enough to adopt a plausible apology for the peculiarities of women. And yet it is a new doctrine that would justify triflers and slanderers. According to this system, it would be absurd to blame those who are perpetually prying into other people's affairs, and industriously blazoning every disadvantageous or suspicious tale.

My dear Madam, you mistake me. Artists may want skill; historians may be partial. Far be it from me to applaud the malignant or the stupid. Ignorance and envy are no favourites of mine, whether they have or have not a chin to be shaved: but nothing would be more grossly absurd, than to suppose these defects to be peculiar to female artists, or the historians of the tea-table. When these defects appear in the most flagrant degree, they are generally capable of an easy apology. If the sexes had, in reality, separate interests, and it were not absurd to set more value on qualifications, on account of their belonging to one of our own sex, it is the women who may justly triumph. Together with power and property, the men have likewise asserted their superior claim to vice and folly.

If I understand you rightly (said the lady), you are of opinion that the sexes are essentially equal.

It appears to me (answered I), that human beings are moulded by the circumstances in which they are placed. In this they are all alike. The differences that flow from the sexual distinction, are as nothing in the balance.

And yet women are often reminded that none of their sex are to be found among the formers of States, and the instructors of mankind—that Pythagoras, Lycurgus, and Socrates, Newton, and Locke, were not women.

True; nor were they mountain savages, nor helots, nor shoemakers. You might as well expect a Laplander to write Greek spontaneously, and without instruction, as that any one should be wise or skillful, without suitable opportunities. I humbly presume one has a better chance of becoming an astronomer by gazing at the stars through a telescope, than in eternally plying the needle, or snapping the scissars. To settle a bill of fare, to lard a pig, to compose a pudding, to carve a goose, are tasks that do not, in any remarkable degree, tend to instil the love, or facilitate the acquisition of literature and science. Nay, I do not form prodigious expectations even of one who reads a novel or comedy once a month, or chants once a day to her harpsichord the hunter's foolish invocation to Phœbus or Cynthia. Women are generally superficial and ignorant, because they are generally cooks and sempstresses. Men are the slaves of habit. It is doubtful whether the career of the species will ever terminate in knowledge. Certain it is, they began in ignorance. Habit has given permanence to errors, which ignorance had previously rendered universal. They are prompt to confound things, which are really distinct; and to persevere in a path to which they have been accustomed. Hence it is that certain employments have been exclusively assigned to women, and that their sex is supposed to disqualify them for any other. Women are defective. They are seldom or never metaphysicians, chemists, or lawgivers. Why? Because they are sempstresses and cooks. This is unavoidable. Such is the unalterable constitution of human nature. They cannot read who never saw an alphabet. They who know no tool but the needle, cannot be skillful at the pen.

Yes (said the lady); of all forms of injustice, that is the most egregious which makes the circumstance of sex a reason for excluding one half of mankind from all those paths which lead to usefulness and honour.

Without doubt (returned I) there is abundance of injustice in the sentence; yet it is possible to misapprehend, and to overrate the injury that flows from the established order of things. If a certain part of every community must be condemned to servile and mechanical professions, it matters not of what sex they may be. If the benefits of leisure and science be, of necessity, the portion of a few, why should we be anxious to which sex the preference is given? The evil lies in so much of human capacity being thus fettered and perverted. This allotment is sad. Perhaps it is unnecessary. Perhaps that precept of justice is practicable, which requires that each man should take his share of the labour, and enjoy his portion of the rest: that the tasks now assigned to a few, might be divided among the whole; and what now degenerates into ceaseless and brutalizing toil, might, by an equitable distribution, be changed into agreeable and useful exercise. Perhaps this inequality is incurable. In either case it is to be lamented, and, as far as possible, mitigated. Now, the question of what sex either of those classes may be composed, is of no importance. Though we must admit the claims of the female sex to an equality with the other, we cannot allow them to be superior. The state of the ignorant, servile, and laborious, is entitled to compassion and relief; not because they are women, nor because they are men; but simply because they are rational.—Among savage nations the women are slaves. They till the ground, and cook the victuals. Such is the condition of half of the community —deplorable, without doubt; but it would be neither more nor less so, if the sexes were equally distributed through each class.

But, the burthen is unequal (said Mrs. Carter), since the strength of the females is less.

What matters it (returned I) whether my strength be much or little, if I am tasked to the amount of it, and no more; and no task can go beyond.

But nature (said the lady) has subjected us to peculiar infirmities and hardships. In consideration of what we

15

suffer as mothers and nurses, I think we ought to be exempted from the same proportion of labour.

It is hard (said I) to determine what is the amount of your pains as mothers and nurses. Have not ease and luxury a tendency to increase that amount? Is not the sustenance of infant offspring in every view a privilege? Of all changes in their condition, that which should transfer to men the task of nurturing the innocence, and helplessness of infancy, would, I should imagine, be to mothers the least acceptable.

I do not complain of this province. It is not, however, exempt from danger and trouble. It makes a large demand upon our time and attention. Ought not this to be considered in the distribution of tasks and duties?

Certainly. I was afraid you would imagine, that too much regard had been paid to it; that the circle of female pursuits had been too much contracted on this account.

I, indeed (rejoined the lady), think it by far too much contracted. But I cannot give the authors of our institutions credit for any such motives. On the contrary, I think we have the highest reason to complain of our exclusion from many professions which might afford us, in common with men, the means of subsistence and independence.

How far, dear Madam, is your complaint well grounded? What is it excludes you from the various occupations in use among us? Cannot a female be a trader? I know no law or custom that forbids it. You may, at any time, draw a subsistence from wages, if your station in life, or your education has rendered you sufficiently robust. No one will deride you, or punish you, for attempting to hew wood or bring water. If we rarely see you driving a team, or beating the anvil, is it not a favorable circumstance? In every family there are various duties. Certainly the most toilsome and rugged do not fall to the lot of women. If your employment be for the most part sedentary and recluse, to be exempted from an intemperate exertion of the muscles, or to be estranged from scenes of vulgar concourse, might be deemed a privilege. The last of these advantages, however, is not yours; for do we not buy most of our meat, herbs, and fruit, of women? In the distribution of employments, the chief or only difference, perhaps, is, that those which require most strength, or more unremitted exertion of it, belong to the males: and yet, there is nothing obligatory or inviolable in this arrangement. In the country, the maid that milks, and the man that ploughs, if discontented with their present office, may make an exchange, without breach of law, or offence to decorum. If you possess stock, by which to purchase the labour of others—and stock may accumulate in your hands as well as in ours—there is no species of manufacture in which you are forbidden to employ it.

But are we not (cried the lady) excluded from the liberal professions?

Why, that may admit of question. You have free access, for example, to the accompting-house. It would be somewhat ludicrous, I own, to see you at the Exchange, or superintending the delivery of a cargo. Yet, this would attract our notice, merely because it is singular; not because it is disgraceful or criminal: but if the singularity be a sufficient objection, we know that these offices are not necessary. The profession of a merchant may be pursued with success and dignity, without being a constant visitor of the quay or the coffee-house. In the trading cities of Europe, there are bankers and merchants of your sex, to whom that consideration is attached, to which they are entitled by their skill, their integrity, or their opulence.

But what apology can you make for our exclusion from the class of physicians?

To a certain extent, the exclusion is imaginary. My grandmother was a tolerable physician. She had much personal experience; and her skill was, I assure you, in much request among her neighbours. It is true, she wisely forbore to tamper with diseases of an uncommon or complicated nature. Her experience was wholly personal. But that was accidental. She might have added, if she had chosen, the experience of others to her own.

But the law—

True, we are not accustomed to see female pleaders at the bar. I never wish to see them there. But the law, as a science, is open to their curiosity, or their benevolence. It may be even practised as a source of gain, without obliging us to frequent and public exhibitions.

Well (said the lady), let us dismiss the lawyer and the physician, and turn our eye to the pulpit. That, at least, is a sanctuary which women must not profane.

It is only (replied I) in some sects that divinity, the business of explaining to men their religious duty, is a trade. In such, custom or law, or the canons of their faith, have confined the pulpit to men: perhaps the distinction, wherever it is found, is an article of their religious creed, and, consequently, is no topic of complaint, since the propriety of this exclusion must be admitted by every member of the sect, whether male or female. But there are other sects which admit females into the class of preachers. With them, indeed, this distinction, if lucrative at all, is only indirectly so; and its profits are not greater to one sex than to the other. But there is no religious society in which women are debarred from the privileges of superior sanctity. The christian religion has done much to level the distinctions of property, and rank, and sex. Perhaps, in reviewing the history of mankind, we shall find the authority derived from a real, or pretended intercourse with heaven, pretty generally divided between them. And after all, what do these restrictions amount to? If some pursuits are monopolized by men, others are appropriated to you. If it appear that your occupations have least of toil, are most friendly to purity of manners, to delicacy of sensation, to intellectual improvement, and activity, or to public usefulness; if it should appear that your skill is always in such demand as to afford you employment when you stand in need of it; if, though few in number, they may be so generally and constantly useful, as always to furnish you subsistence; or, at least, to expose you, by their vicissitudes, to the pressure of want as rarely as it is incident to men; you cannot reasonably complain: but, in my opinion, all this is true.

Perhaps not (replied the lady): yet I must own your statement is plausible. I shall not take much pains to confute it. It is evident, that, for some reason or other, the liberal professions, those which require most vigour of mind, greatest extent of knowledge, and most commerce with books and with enlightened society, are occupied only by men. If contrary instances occur, they are rare, and must be considered as exceptions.

Admitting these facts (said I), I do not see reason for drawing mortifying inferences from them. For my part, I entertain but little respect for what are called the liberal professions, and, indeed, but little for any profession whatever. If their motive be gain, and that it is which constitutes them a profession, they seem to be, all of them, nearly on a level in point of dignity. The consideration of usefulness is of more value. He that roots out a national vice, or checks the ravages of a pestilence, is, no doubt, a respectable personage: but it is no man's trade to perform these services. How does a mercenary divine, or lawyer, or physician, differ from a dishonest chimney-sweep? The most that can be dreaded from a chimney-sweep is the spoiling of our dinner, or a little temporary alarm; but what injuries may we not dread from the abuses of law, medicine, or divinity! Honesty, you will say, is the best policy. Whatever it be, it is not the road to wealth. To the purposes of a profession, as such, it is not subservient. Degrees, and examinations, and licences, may qualify us for the trade; but benevolence needs not their aid to refine its skill, or augment its activity. Some portion of their time and their efforts must be employed by those who need, in obtaining the means of subsistence. The less tiresome, boisterous and servile that task is, which necessity enjoins; the less tendency it has to harden our hearts, to benumb our intellects, to undermine our health. The more leisure it affords us to gratify our curiosity and cultivate our moral discernment, the better. Here is a criterion for the choice of a profession, and which obliges us to consider the condition of women as preferable.

I cannot perceive it. But it matters nothing what field may be open, if our education does not qualify us to range over it. What think you of female education? Mine has been frivolous. I can make a pie, and cut out a gown. For this only I am indebted to my teachers. If I have added any thing to these valuable attainments, it is through my own efforts, and not by the assistance or encouragement of others.

And ought it not to be so? What can render men wise but their own efforts? Does curiosity derive no encouragement from the possession of the power and materials? You are taught to read and to write: quills, paper, and books are at hand. Instruments and machines are forthcoming to those who can purchase them. If you be insensible to the pleasures and benefits of knowledge, and are therefore ignorant and trifling, it is not for want of assistance and encouragement.

I shall find no difficulty (said the lady) to admit that the system is not such as to condemn all women, without exception, to stupidity. As it is, we have only to lament, that a sentence so unjust is executed on, by far, the greater number. But you forget how seldom those who are most fortunately situated, are permitted to cater for themselves. Their conduct, in this case, as in all others, is subject to the controul of others who are guided by established prejudices, and are careful to remember that we are women. They think a being of this sex is to be instructed in a manner different from those of another. Schools, and colleges, and public instructors are provided in all the abstruse sciences and learned languages; but whatever may be their advantages, are not women totally excluded from them?

It would be prudent (said I), in the first place, to ascertain the amount of those advantages, before we indulge ourselves in lamenting the loss of them. Let us consider whether a public education be not unfavourable to moral and intellectual improvement; or, at least, whether it be preferable to the domestic method;—whether most knowledge be obtained by listening to hired professors, or by reading books;—whether the abstruse sciences be best studied in a closet, or a college;—whether the ancient tongues be worth learning;—whether, since languages are of no use but as avenues to knowledge, our native tongue, especially in its present state of refinement, be not the best. Before we lament the exclusion of women from colleges, all these points must be settled: unless they shall be precluded by reflecting, that places of public education, which are colleges in all respects but the name, are, perhaps, as numerous for females as for males.

They differ (said the lady) from colleges in this, that a very different plan of instruction is followed. I know of no female school where Latin is taught, or geometry, or chemistry.

Yet, Madam, there are female geometricians, and chemists, and scholars, not a few. Were I desirous that my son or daughter should become either of these, I should not deem the assistance of a college indispensible. Suppose an anatomist should open a school to pupils of both sexes, and solicit equally their attendance; would you comply with the invitation?

No; because that pursuit has no attractions for me. But if I had a friend whose curiosity was directed to it, why should I dissuade her from it?

Perhaps (said I) you are but little acquainted with the real circumstances of such a scene. If your disdain of prejudices should prompt you to adventure one visit, I question whether you would find an inclination to repeat it.

Perhaps not (said she); but that mode of instruction in all the experimental sciences is not, perhaps, the best. A numerous company can derive little benefit from a dissection in their presence. A closer and more deliberate inspection than the circumstances of a large company will allow, seems requisite. But the assembly need not be a mixed one. Objections on the score of delicacy, though they are more specious than sound, and owe their force more to our weakness than our wisdom, would be removed by making the whole company, professor and pupils, female. But this would be obviating an imaginary evil, at the price of a real benefit. Nothing has been more injurious than the separation of the sexes. They associate in childhood without restraint; but the period quickly arrives when they are obliged to take different paths. Ideas, maxims, and pursuits, wholly opposite, engross their attention. Different systems of morality, different languages, or, at least, the same words with a different set of meanings, are adopted. All intercourse between them is fettered and embarrassed. On one side, all is reserve and artifice. On the other, adulation and affected humility. The same end must be compassed by opposite means. The man must affect a disproportionable ardour; while the woman must counterfeit indifference and aversion. Her tongue has no office, but to belie the sentiments of her heart, and the dictates of her understanding.

By marriage she loses all right to separate property. The will of her husband is the criterion of all her duties. All merit is comprised in unlimited obedience. She must not expostulate or rebel. In all contests with him, she must hope to prevail by blandishments and tears; not by appeals to justice and addresses to reason. She will be most applauded when she smiles with most perseverence on her oppressor, and when, with the undistinguishing attachment of a dog, no caprice or cruelty shall be able to estrange her affection.

Surely, Madam, this picture is exaggerated. You derive it from some other source than your own experience, or even your own observation.

No; I believe the picture to be generally exact. No doubt there are exceptions. I believe myself to be one. I think myself exempt from the grosser defects of women; but by no means free from the influence of a mistaken education. But why should you think the picture exaggerated? Man is the strongest. This is the reason why, in the earliest stage of society, the females are slaves. The tendency of rational improvement is to equalize conditions; to abolish all distinctions, but those that are founded in truth and reason; to limit the reign of brute force, and uncontroulable accidents. Women have unquestionably benefited by the progress that has hitherto taken place. If I look abroad, I may see reason to congratulate myself on being born in this age and country. Women, that are no where totally exempt from servitude, no where admitted to their true rank in society, may yet be subject to different degrees or kinds of servitude. Perhaps there is no country in the world where the yoke is lighter than here. But this persuasion, though, in one view, it may afford us consolation, ought not to blind us to our true condition, or weaken our efforts to remove the evils that still oppress us. It is manifest, that we are hardly and unjustly treated. The natives of the most distant regions do not less resemble each other, than the male and female of the same tribe, in consequence of the different discipline to which they are subject. Now, this is palpably absurd. Men and women are partakers of the same nature. They are rational beings; and, as such, the same principles of truth and equity must be applicable to both.

To this I replied, Certainly, Madam: but it is obvious to inquire to which of the sexes the distinction is most favourable. In some respects, different paths are allotted to them, but I am apt to suspect that of the woman to be strewed with fewest thorns; to be beset with fewest asperities; and to lead, if not absolutely in conformity to truth and equity, yet with fewest deviations from it. There are evils incident to your condition as women. As human beings, we all lie under considerable disadvantages; but it is of an unequal lot that you complain. The institutions of society have injuriously and capriciously distinguished you. True it is, laws, which have commonly been male births, have treated you unjustly; but it has been with that species of injustice that has given birth to nobles and kings. They have distinguished you by irrational and undeserved indulgences. They have exempted you from a thousand toils and cares. Their tenderness has secluded you from tumult and noise: your persons are sacred from profane violences; your eyes from ghastly spectacles; your ears from a thousand discords, by which ours are incessantly invaded. Yours are the peacefullest recesses of the mansion: your hours glide along in sportive chat, in harmless recreation, or voluptuous indolence; or in labour so light, as scarcely to be termed encroachments on the reign of contemplation. Your industry delights in the graceful and minute: it enlarges the empire of the senses, and improves the flexibility of the fibres. The art of the needle, by the lustre of its hues and the delicacy of its touches, is able to mimic all the forms of nature, and pourtray all the images of fancy: and the needle but prepares the hand for doing wonders on the harp; for conjuring up the 'piano' to melt, and the 'forte' to astound us.

This (cried the lady) is a very partial description. It can apply only to the opulent, and but to few of them. Meanwhile, how shall we estimate the hardships of the lower class? You have only pronounced a panegyric on indolence and luxury. Eminent virtue and true happiness are not to be found in this element.

True (returned I). I have only attempted to justify the male sex from the charge of cruelty. Ease and luxury are pernicious. Kings and nobles, the rich and the idle, enjoy no genuine content. Their lot is hard enough; but still it is better than brutal ignorance and unintermitted toil; than nakedness and hunger. There must be one condition of society that approaches nearer than any other to the standard of rectitude and happiness. For this it is our duty to search; and, having found it, endeavour to reduce every other condition to this desirable mean. It is useful, meanwhile, to ascertain the relative importance of different conditions; and since deplorable evils are annexed to every state, to discover in what respects, and in what degree, one is more or less eligible than another. Half of the community are females. Let the whole community be divided into classes; and let us inquire, whether the wives, and daughters, and single women, of each class, be not placed in a more favourable situation than the husbands, sons, and single men, of the same class. Our answer will surely be in the affirmative.

There is (said the lady) but one important question relative to this subject. Are women as high in the scale of social felicity and usefulness as they may and ought to be?

To this (said I) there can be but one answer: No. At present they are only higher on that scale than the men. You will observe, Madam, I speak only of that state of society which we enjoy. If you had excluded sex from the question, I must have made the same answer. Human beings, it is to be hoped, are destined to a better condition on this stage, or some other, than is now allotted them.

PART II

This remark was succeeded by a pause on both sides. The lady seemed more inclined to listen than talk. At length I ventured to resume the conversation.

Pray, Madam, permit me to return from this impertinent digression, and repeat my question—"Are you a federalist?"

And let me (replied she) repeat my answer—What have I, as a woman, to do with politics? Even the government of our country, which is said to be the freest in the world, passes over women as if they were not. We are excluded from all political rights without the least ceremony. Lawmakers thought as little of comprehending us in their code of liberty, as if we were pigs, or sheep. That females are exceptions to their general maxims, perhaps never occurred to them. If it did, the idea was quietly discarded, without leaving behind the slightest consciousness of inconsistency or injustice. If to uphold and defend, as far as woman's little power extends, the constitution, against violence; if to prefer a scheme of union and confederacy, to war and dissention, entitle me to that name, I may justly be stiled a federalist. But if that title be incompatible with a belief that, in many particulars, this constitution is unjust and absurd, I certainly cannot pretend to it. But how should it be otherwise? While I am conscious of being an intelligent and moral being; while I see myself denied, in so many cases, the exercise of my own discretion; incapable of separate property; subject, in all periods of my life, to the will of another, on whose bounty I am made to depend for food, raiment, and shelter: when I see myself, in my relation to society, regarded merely as a beast, or an insect; passed over, in the distribution of public duties, as absolutely nothing, by those who disdain to assign the least apology for their injustice —what though politicians say I am nothing, it is impossible I should assent to their opinion, as long as I am conscious of willing and moving. If they generously admit me into the class of existence, but affirm that I exist for no purpose but the convenience of the more dignified sex; that I am not to be entrusted with the government of myself; that to foresee, to deliberate and decide, belongs to others, while all my duties resolve themselves into this precept, "listen and obey;" it is not for me to smile at their tyranny, or receive, as my gospel, a code built upon such atrocious maxims. No, I am no federalist.

You are, at least (said I), a severe and uncommon censor. You assign most extraordinary reasons for your political heresy. You have many companions in your aversion to the government, but, I suspect, are wholly singular in your motives. There are few, even among your own sex, who reason in this manner.

Very probably; thoughtless and servile creatures! but that is not wonderful. All despotism subsists by virtue of the errors and supineness of its slaves. If their discernment was clear, their persons would be free. Brute strength has no part in the government of multitudes: they are bound in the fetters of opinion.

The maxims of constitution-makers sound well. All

power is derived from the people. Liberty is every one's birthright. Since all cannot govern or deliberate individually, it is just that they should elect their representatives. That every one should possess, indirectly, and through the medium of his representatives, a voice in the public councils; and should yield to no will but that of an actual or virtual majority. Plausible and specious maxims! but fallacious. What avails it to be told by any one, that he is an advocate for liberty? we must first know what he means by the word. We shall generally find that he intends only freedom to himself, and subjection to all others. Suppose I place myself where I can conveniently mark the proceedings at a general election: "All," says the code, "are free. Liberty is the immediate gift of the Creator to all mankind, and is unalienable. Those that are subject to the laws should possess a share in their enaction. This privilege can be exercised, consistently with the maintenance of social order, in a large society, only in the choice of deputies." A person advances with his ticket. "Pray," says the officer, "are you twenty-one years of age?"—"No."—"Then I cannot receive your vote; you are no citizen." Disconcerted and abashed, he retires. A second assumes his place. "How long," says the officer, "have you been an inhabitant of this State?" —"Nineteen months and a few days."—"None has a right to vote who has not completed two years residence." A third approaches, who is rejected because his name is not found in the catalogue of taxables. At length room is made for a fourth person. "Man," cries the magistrate, "is your skin black or white?"—"Black."—"What, a sooty slave dare to usurp the rights of freemen?" The way being now clear, I venture to approach. "I am not a minor," say I to myself. "I was born in the State, and cannot, therefore, be stigmatized as a foreigner. I pay taxes, for I have no father or husband to pay them for me. Luckily my complexion is white. Surely my vote will be received. But, no, I am a woman. Neither short residence, nor poverty, nor age, nor colour, nor sex, exempt from the jurisdiction of the laws." "True," says the magistrate; "but they deprive you from bearing any part in their formation." "So I perceive, but I cannot perceive the justice of your pretentions to equality and liberty, when those principles are thus openly and grossly violated."

If a stranger question me concerning the nature of our government, I answer, that in this happy climate all men are free: the people are the source of all authority; from them it flows, and to them, in due season, it returns. But in what (says my friend) does this unrivalled and precious freedom consist? Not (say I) in every man's governing himself, literally and individually; that is impossible. Not in the controul of an actual majority; they are by much too numerous to deliberate commodiously, or decide expeditiously. No, our liberty consists in the choice of our governors: all, as reason requires, have a part in this choice, yet not without a few exceptions; for, in the first place, all females are excepted. They, indeed, compose one half of the community; but, no matter, women cannot possibly have any rights. Secondly, those whom the feudal law calls minors, because they could not lift a shield, or manage a pike, are excepted. They comprehend one half of the remainder. Thirdly, the poor. These vary in number, but are sure to increase with the increase of luxury and opulence, and to promote these is well known to be the aim of all wise governors. Fourthly, those who have not been two years in the land : and, lastly, slaves. It has been sagely decreed, that none but freemen shall enjoy this privilege, and that all men are free but those that are slaves. When all these are sifted out, a majority of the remainder are entitled to elect our governor; provided, however, the candidate possess certain qualifications, which you will excuse me from enumerating. I am tired of explaining this charming system of equality and independence. Let the black, the young, the poor, and the stranger, support their own claims. I am a woman. As such, I cannot celebrate the equity of that scheme of government which classes me with dogs and swine.

In this representation (said I) it must be allowed there is some truth; but do you sufficiently distinguish between the form and spirit of a government? The true condition of a nation cannot be described in a few words; nor can it be found in the volumes of their laws. We know little or nothing when our knowledge extends no farther than the forms of the constitution. As to any direct part they bear in the government, the women of Turky, Russia, and America, are alike; but, surely, their actual condition, their dignity, and freedom, are very different. The value

33

of any government lies in the mode in which it is exercised. If we consent to be ruled by another, our liberty may still remain inviolate, or be infringed only when superior wisdom directs. Our master may govern us agreeably to our own ideas, or may restrain and enforce us only when our own views are mistaken.

No government is independent of popular opinion. By that it must necessarily be sustained and modified. In the worst despotism there is a sphere of discretion allotted to each man, which political authority must not violate. How much soever is relinquished by the people, somewhat is always reserved. The chief purpose of the wise is to make men their own governors, to persuade them to practise the rules of equity without legal constraint: they will try to lessen the quantity of government, without changing or multiplying the depositories of it; to diminish the number of those cases in which authority is required to interfere. We need not complain of the injustice of laws, if we refrain, or do not find it needful to appeal to them: if we decide amicably our differences, or refer them to an umpire of our own choice: if we trust not to the subtilty of lawyers, and the prejudice of judges, but to our own eloquence, and a tribunal of our neighbours. It matters not what power the laws give me over the property or persons of others, if I do not chuse to avail myself of the privilege.

Then (said the lady) you think that forms of government are no subjects of contest. It matters not by whom power is possessed, or how it is transferred; whether we bestow our allegiance on a child or a lunatic; whether kings be made by the accident of birth or wealth; whether supreme power be acquired by force, or transmitted by inheritance, or conferred freely and periodically by the suffrages of all that acknowledge its validity?

Doubtless (replied I) these considerations are of some moment; but cannot you distinguish between power and the exercise of power, and see that the importance of the first is derived wholly from the consideration of the last?

But how it shall be exercised (rejoined she) depends wholly on the views and habits of him that has it. Avails it nothing whether the prince be mild or austere, malignant or benevolent? If we must delegate authority, are we not concerned to repose it with him who will use it to the best, rather than the worst purposes? True it is, we should retain as much power over our own conduct, maintain the sphere of our own discretion, as large and as inviolate as possible. But we must, as long as we associate with mankind, forego, in some particulars, our self-government, and submit to the direction of another; but nothing interests me more nearly than a wise choice of a master. The wisest member of society should, if possible, be selected for the guidance of the rest.

If an hundred persons be in want of a common dwelling, and the work cannot be planned or executed by the whole, from the want of either skill or unanimity, what is to be done? We must search out one who will do that which the circumstances of the case will not allow us to do for our selves. Is it not obvious to inquire who among us possesses most skill, and most virtue to controul him in the use of it? Or shall we lay aside all regard to skill and integrity, and consider merely who is the tallest, or richest, or fairest among us, or admit his title that can prove that such an one was his father, or that he himself is the eldest among the children of his father? In an affair which is of common concern, shall we consign the province of deciding to a part, or yield to the superior claims of a majority? If it happen that the smaller number be distinguished by more accurate discernment, or extensive knowledge, and, consequently, he that is chosen by the wiser few, will probably be, in himself, considered more worthy than the favourite of the injudicious many; yet what is the criterion which shall enable us to distinguish the sages from the fools? And, when the selection is made, what means shall we use for expunging from the catalogue all those whom age has enfeebled, or flattery or power corrupted? If all this were effected, could we, at the same time, exclude evils from our system, by which its benefits would be overweighed? Of all modes of government, is not the sovereignty of the people, however incumbered with inconveniencies, yet attended by the fewest?

It is true (answered I) that one form of government may tend more than another to generate selfishness and tyranny in him that rules, and ignorance and profligacy in the subjects. If different forms be submitted to our choice, we should elect that which deserves the preference. Suppose our countrymen would be happier if they were subdivided into a thousand little independent democratical republics, than they are under their present form, or than they would be under an hereditary despot: then it behoves us to inquire by what, if by any means, this subdivision may be effected, and, which is matter of equal moment, how it can be maintained: but these, for the most part, are airy speculations. If not absolutely hurtful, they are injurious, by being of inferior utility to others which they exclude. If women be excluded from political functions, it is sufficient that, in this exercise of these functions, their happiness is amply consulted.

Say what you will (cried the lady), I shall ever consider it as a gross abuse that we are hindered from sharing with you in the power of chusing our rulers, and of making those laws to which we equally with yourselves are subject.

We claim the power (rejoined I); this cannot be denied; but I must maintain, that as long as it is equitably exercised, no alteration is desirable. Shall the young, the poor, the stranger, and the females, be admitted, indiscriminately, to political privileges? Shall we annex no condition to a voter but that he be a thing in human shape, not lunatic, and capable of locomotion; and no qualifications to a candidate but the choice of a majority? Would any benefit result from the change? Will it augment the likelihood that the choice will fall upon the wisest? Will it endow the framers and interpreters of law with more sagacity and moderation than they at present possess?

Perhaps not (said she). I plead only for my own sex. Want of property, youth, and servile condition, may, possibly, be well-founded objections; but mere sex is a circumstance so purely physical; has so little essential influence beyond what has flowed from the caprice of civil institutions on the qualities of mind or person, that I cannot think of it without impatience. If the law should exclude from all political functions every one who had a mole on his right cheek, or whose stature did not exceed five feet six inches, who would not condemn, without scruple, so unjust an institution? yet, in truth, the injustice would be less than in the case of women. The distinction is no less futile, but the injury is far greater, since it annihilates the political existence of at least one half of the community.

But you appeared to grant (said I) that want of property and servile condition are allowable disqualifications. Now, may not marriage be said to take away both the liberty and property of women? at least, does it not bereave them of that independent judgment which it is just to demand from a voter?

Not universally the property (answered she): so far as it has the effect you mention, was there ever any absurdity more palpable, any injustice more flagrant? But you well know there are cases in which women, by marriage, do not relinquish their property. All women, however, are not wives and wards. Granting that such are disqualified, what shall we say of those who are indisputably single, affluent and independent? Against these no objection, in the slightest degree plausible, can be urged. It would be strange folly to suppose women of this class to be necessarily destitute of those qualities which the station of citizen requires. We have only to examine the pretentions of those who already occupy public stations. Most of them seem not to have attained heights inaccessible to ordinary understandings; and yet the delegation of women, however opulent and enlightened, would, probably, be a more insupportable shock to the prejudices that prevail among us, than the appointment of a youth of fifteen, or a beggar, or a stranger.

If this innovation be just (said I), the period for making it has not arrived. You, Madam, are singular. Women in general do not reason in this manner. They are contented with the post assigned them. If the rights of a citizen were extended to them, they would not employ them—stay till they desire it.

If they were wise (returned the lady), they would desire it: meanwhile, it is an act of odious injustice to withhold it. This privilege is their due. By what means have you discovered that they would not exercise it, if it were granted? You cannot imagine but that some would step forth and occupy this station, when the obstruction was removed.

I know little of women (said I); I have seldom approached them, much less have I enjoyed their intimate society; yet, as a specimen of the prejudice you spoke of, I must own I should be not a little surprised to hear of a woman proferring her services as president or senator. It would be hard to restrain a smile to see her rise in a popular assembly to discuss some mighty topic. I should gaze as at a prodigy, and listen with a doubting heart: yet I might not refuse devotion to the same woman in the character of household deity. As a mother, pressing a charming babe to her bosom; as my companion in the paths of love, or poetry, or science; as partaker with me in content, and an elegant sufficiency, her dignity would shine forth in full splendour. Here all would be decency and grace. But as a national ruler; as busied in political intrigues and cares; as intrenched in the paper mounds of a secretary; as burthened with the gravity of a judge; as bearing the standard in battle; or, even as a champion in senatorial warfare, it would be difficult to behold her without regret and disapprobation. These emotions I should not pretend to justify; but such, and so difficult to vanquish, is prejudice.

Prejudices, countenanced by an experience so specious and universal, cannot be suddenly subdued. I shall tell you, however, my genuine and deliberate opinion on the subject. I have said that the equality of the sexes was all that could be admitted; that the superiority we deny to men can, with as little justice, be ascribed to women: but this, in the strictest sense, is not true: on the contrary, it must be allowed that women are superior.

We cannot fail to distinguish between the qualities of mind and those of person. Whatever be the relation between the thinking principle, and the limbs and organs of the body, it is manifest that they are distinct; insomuch, that when we pass judgment on the qualities of the former, the latter is not necessarily taken into view, or included in it. So, when we discourse of our exterior and sensible qualities, we are supposed to exclude from our present consideration, the endowments of the mind. This distinction is loose, but sufficiently accurate for my purpose.

Have we not abundant reason to conclude that the principle of thought is, in both sexes, the same; that it is subject to like influences; that like motives and situations produce like effects? We are not concerned to know which of the sexes has occupied the foremost place on the stage of human life. They would not be beings of the same nature in whom different causes produced like effects. It is sufficient that we can trace diversity in the effects to a corresponding diversity in the circumstances; that women are such as observation exhibits them, in consequence of those laws which belong to a rational being, and which are common to both sexes: but such, beyond all doubt, must be the result of our inquiries. In this respect, then, the sexes are equal.

But what opinion must be formed of their exterior or personal qualities? Are not the members and organs of the female body as aptly suited to their purposes as those of the male? The same, indeed, may be asserted of a mouse or a grasshopper; but are not these purposes as wise and dignified, nay, are they not precisely the same? Considering the female frame as the subject of impressions, and the organ of intelligence, it appears to deserve the preference. What shall we say of the acuteness and variety of your sensations; of the smoothness, flexibility, and compass of your voice?

Beauty is a doubtful quality. Few men will scruple to resign the superiority in this respect to women. The truth of this decision may be, perhaps, physically demonstrated; or, perhaps, all our reasonings are vitiated, by this circumstance, that the reasoner and his auditors are male. We all know in what the sexual distinction consists, and what is the final cause of this distinction. It is easier to conceive than describe that species of attraction which sex annexes to the person. It would be fallacious, perhaps, to infer female superiority, in an absolute and general sense, from the devotion which, in certain cases, we are prone to pay them; which it is impossible to feel for one of our own sex; and which is mutually felt: yet, methinks, the inference is inevitable. When I reflect on the equality of mind, and attend to the feelings which are roused in my bosom by the presence of accomplished and lovely women; by the mere graces of their exterior, even when the magic of their voice sleeps, and the eloquence of their eyes is mute;—and, for the reality of these feelings, if politeness did not forbid, I might quote the experience of the present moment—I am irresistibly induced to believe, that, of the two sexes, yours is, on the whole, superior.

It is difficult, I know, to reason dispassionately on this subject: witness the universal persuasion of mankind, that in grace, symmetry, and melody, the preference is due to women. Yet, beside that opinion is no criterion of truth but to him that harbours it, when I call upon all human kind as witnesses, it is only one half of them, the individuals of one sex, that obey my call.

It may at first appear that men have generally ascribed intellectual pre-eminence to themselves. Nothing, however, can be inferred from this. It is doubtful whether they judge rightly on the question of what is or is not intrinsically excellent. Not seldom they have placed their superiority in that which, rightly understood, should have been pregnant with ignominy and humiliation. Should women themselves be found to concur in this belief, that the other sex surpasses them in intelligence, it will avail but little. We must still remember that opinion is evidence of nothing but its own existence. This opinion, indeed, is peculiarly obnoxious. They merely repeat what they have been taught; and their teachers have been men. The prevalence of this opinion, if it does not evince the incurable defects of female capacity, may, at least, be cited to prove in how mournful a degree that capacity has been neglected or perverted. It is a branch of that prejudice which has so long darkened the world, and taught men that nobles and kings were creatures of an order superior to themselves.

Here the conversation was interrupted by one of the company, who, after listening to us for some time, thought proper at last to approach, and contribute his mite to our mutual edification. I soon after seized an opportunity of withdrawing, but not without requesting and obtaining permission to repeat my visit.

PARTS III & IV

A week elapsed and I repeated my visit to Mrs. Carter. She greeted me in a friendly manner. I have often, said she, since I saw you, reflected on the subject of our former conversation. I have meditated more deeply than common, and I believe to more advantage. The hints that you gave me I have found useful guides.

And I, said I, have travelled farther than common, incited by a laudable desire of knowledge.

Travelled?

Yes, I have visited since I saw you, the paradise of women; and I assure you have longed for an opportunity to communicate the information that I have collected.

Well: you now enjoy the opportunity; you have engaged it every day in the week. Whenever you had thought proper to come, I could have promised you a welcome.

I thank you. I should have claimed your welcome sooner, but only returned this evening.

Returned! Whence, I pry'thee?

From the journey that I spoke of. Have I not told you that I have visited the paradise of women? The region, indeed is far distant, but a twinkling is sufficient for the longest of my journeys.

You are somewhat mysterious, and mystery is one of the many things that abound in the world, for which I have an hearty aversion.

I cannot help it. It is plain enough to me and to my good genius, who when I am anxious to change the scene, and am unable to perform it by the usual means, is kindly present to my prayers, and saves me from three inconveniences, of travelling toil, delay and expense. What sort of vehicle it is that he provides for me, what intervals of space I have overpassed, and what is the situation of the inn where I repose, relatively to this city or this orb, such is the rapidity with which I move that I cannot collect from my own observation. I may sometimes remedy my ignorance in this respect by a comparison of circumstances; for example, the language of the people with whom I passed most of the last week, was English. This was a strong symptom of affinity. In other respects the resemblance was sufficiently obscure. Methought I could trace in their buildings the knowledge of Greek and Roman models: but who can tell that the same images and combinations may not occur to minds distant and unacquainted with each other, but which have been subject to the same enlightened discipline? In manners and sentiments they possessed little in common with us. Here I confess my wonder was most excited, I should have been apt to suspect that they were people of some other planet, especially as I had never met in my reading with any intimations of the existence of such a people on our own. But on looking around me the earth and sky exhibited the same appearances as with us. It once occurred to me, that I had passed the bourne which we are all doomed to pass, and had reached that spot from which, as the poet assures us, no traveller returns. But since I have returned, I must discard that supposition. You will say perhaps when you are acquainted with particulars that it was no more than a sick man's dream, or a poet's reverie. Though I myself cannot adopt this opinion, for who can discredit the testimony of his senses, yet it must be owned that it would most naturally suggest itself to another, and therefore I shall leave you in possession of it.

So, you would persuade me, said the lady, that the journey you meant to relate, is in your own opinion real, though you are conscious that its improbability will hinder others from believing it.

If my statement answer that end be it so. The worst judge of the nature of his own conceptions is the enthusiast: I have my portion of ardour which solitude seldom fails to kindle into blaze. It has drawn vigour and activity from exercise. Whether it transgress the limits which a correct judgment prescribes it would be absurd to inquire of the enthusiast himself. If the perceptions of the poet be as lively as those of sense, it is a superfluous inquiry whether their objects exist really, and externally. This is a question which cannot be decided, even with respect to those perceptions which have most seeming and most congruity. We have no direct proof that the ordinary objects of sight and touch have a being independent of these senses. When there is no ground for believing that those chairs and tables have any existence but in my own sensorium, it would be rash to affirm the reality of the objects which I met, or seemed to meet with in my late journey. I see and hear is the utmost that can be truly said at any time, all that I can say is, that I saw and heard.

Well, returned the lady, that as you say, is a point of small importance. Let me know what you saw and heard without further ceremony.

I was witness to the transactions of a people, who would probably gain more of your approbation than those around you can hope for. Yet this is perhaps to build too largely on my imperfect knowledge of your sentiments: however that be, few things offered themselves to my observation, which I did not see reason to applaud, and to wonder at.

My curiosity embraced an ample field. It did not over-look the condition of women. That negligence had been equally unworthy of my understanding and my heart. It was evening and the moon was present when I lighted, I know not how or whence, on a smooth pavement en-compassed by structures that appeared intended for the accommodation of those whose taste led them either to studious retirement or to cheerful conversation. I shall not describe the first transports of my amazement, or dwell on the reflections that were suggested by a transi-tion so new and uncommon, or the means that I em-ployed to penetrate the mysteriousness that hung around every object, and my various conjectures as to the position of the Isle, or the condition of the people among whom I had fallen. I need not tell how in wandering from this spot, I encountered many of both sexes who were em-ployed in awakening by their notes, the neighbouring echoes, or absorbed in musing silence, or engaged in sprightly debate; how one of them remarking as I suppose, the perplexity of my looks, and the uncouthness of my garb, accosted me and condescended to be my guide in a devious tract, which conducted me from one scene of enchantment to another. I need not tell how by the aid of this benevolent conductor, I passed through halls whose pendent lustres exhibited sometimes a groupe of musicians and dancers, sometimes assemblies where state affairs were the theme of sonorous rhetoric, where the claims of ancient patriots and heroes to the veneration of posterity were examined, and the sources of memorable revolutions scrutinized, or which listened to the rehearsals of annalist or poet, or surveyed the labours of the chemist, or inspected the performances of the mechanical inventor. Need I expatiate on the felicity of that plan, which blended the umbrage of poplars with the murmur of fountains, enhanced by the gracefulness of architecture.

Come, come, interrupted the lady, this perhaps, may be poetry, but though pleasing it had better be dispensed with. I give you leave to pass over these incidents in silence: I desire merely to obtain the sum of your information, disembarrassed from details of the mode in which you acquired it, and of the mistakes and conjectures to which your ignorance subjected you.

Well, said I, these restraints it must be owned are a little hard, but since you are pleased to impose them I must conform to your pleasure. After my curiosity was sufficiently gratified by what was to be seen, I retired with my guide to his apartment. It was situated on a terrace which overlooked a mixed scene of groves and edifices, which the light of the moon that had now ascended the meridian, had rendered distinctly visible. After considerable discourse, in which satisfactory answers had been made to all the inquiries which I had thought proper to make, I ventured to ask, I pray thee my good friend, what is the condition of the female sex among you? In this evening's excursion I have met with those, whose faces and voices seemed to bespeak them women, though as far as I could discover they were distinguished by no peculiarities of manners or dress. In those assemblies to which you conducted me, I did not fail to observe that whatever was the business of the hour, both sexes seemed equally engaged in it. Was the spectacle theatrical? The stage was occupied sometimes by men, sometimes by women, and sometimes by a company of each. The tenor of the drama seemed to be followed as implicitly as if custom had enacted no laws upon this subject. Their voices were mingled in the chorusses: I admired the order in which the spectators were arranged. Women were, to a certain degree, associated with women, and men with men; but it seemed as if magnificence and symmetry had been consulted, rather than a scrupulous decorum. Here no distinction in dress was observable, but I suppose the occasion dictated it. Was science or poetry, or art, the topic of discussion? The two sexes mingled their inquiries and opinions. The debate was managed with ardour and freedom, and all present were admitted to a share in the controversy, without particular exceptions or compliances of any sort.

Were shadows and recesses sought by the studious few? As far as their faces were distinguishable, meditation had selected her votaries indiscriminately. I am not unaccustomed to some degree of this equality among my own countrymen, but it appears to be far more absolute and general among you; pray what are your customs and institutions on this head?

Perhaps, replied my friend, I do not see whither your question tends. What are our customs respecting women? You are doubtless apprised of the difference that subsists between the sexes. That physical constitution which entitles some of us to the appellation of male, and others to that of female you must know. You know its consequences. With these our customs and institutions have no concern; they result from the order of nature, which it is our business merely to investigate. I suppose there are physiologists or anatomists in your country. To them it belongs to explain this circumstance of animal existence.

The universe consists of individuals. They are perishable. Provision has been made that the place of those that perish should be supplied by new generations. The means by which this end is accomplished, are the same through every tribe of animals. Between contemporary beings the distinction of sex maintains; but the end of this distinction is that since each individual must perish, there may be a continual succession of individuals. If you seek to know more than this, I must refer you to books which contain the speculations of the anatomist, or to the hall where he publicly communicates his doctrines.

It is evident, answered I, that I have not made myself understood. I did not inquire into the structure of the human body, but into these moral or political maxims which are founded on the difference in this structure between the sexes.

Need I repeat, said my friend, what I have told you of the principles by which we are governed. I am aware that there are nations of men universally infected by error, or who at least entertain opinions different from ours. It is hard to trace all the effects of a particular belief, which chances to be current among a whole people. I have entered into a pretty copious explanation of the rules to which we conform in our intercourse with each other, but still perhaps have been deficient.

No, I cannot complain of your brevity; perhaps my doubts would be solved by reflecting attentively on the information that I have already received. For that, leisure is requisite; meanwhile I cannot but confess my surprise that I find among you none of those exterior differences by which the sexes are distinguished by all other nations.

Give me a specimen if you please, of those differences with which you have been familiar.

One of them, said I, is dress. Each sex has a garb peculiar to itself. The men and women of our country are more different from each other in this respect, than the natives of remotest countries.

That is strange, said my friend, why is it so?

I know not. Each one dresses as custom prescribes. He has no other criterion. If he selects his garb because it is beautiful or convenient, it is beautiful and commodious in his eyes merely because it is customary.

But wherefore does custom prescribe a different dress to each sex?

I confess I cannot tell, but most certainly it is so. I must likewise acknowledge that nothing in your manners more excites my surprise than your uniformity in this particular.

Why should it be inexplicable? For what end do we dress? Is it for the sake of ornament? Is it in compliance with our perceptions of the beautiful? These perceptions cannot be supposed to be the same in all. But since the standard of beauty whatever it be, must be one and the same: since our notions on this head are considerably affected by custom and example, and since all have nearly the same opportunities and materials of judgment, if beauty only were regarded, the differences among us would be trivial. Differences, perhaps, there would be. The garb of one being would, in some degree, however small, vary from that of another. But what causes there are that should make all women agree in their preference of one dress, and all men in that of another, is utterly incomprehensible; no less than that the difference resulting from this choice should be essential and conspicuous.

But ornament obtains no regard from us but in subservience to utility. We find it hard to distinguish between the useful and beautiful. When they appear to differ, we cannot hesitate to prefer the former. To us that instrument possesses an invincible superiority to every other which is best adapted to our purpose. Convince me that this garment is of more use than that, and you have determined my choice. We may afterwards inquire, which has the highest pretensions to beauty. Strange if utility and beauty fail to coincide. Stranger still, if having found them in any instance compatible, I sacrifice the former to the latter. But the elements of beauty, though perhaps they have a real existence, are fleeting and inconstant. Not so those principles which enable us to discover what is useful. These are uniform and permanent. So must be the results. Among us, what is useful to one, must be equally so to another. The condition of all is so much alike, that a stuff which deserves the preference of one, because it is obtained with least labour, because its texture is most durable, or most easily renewed or cleansed, is for similar reasons, preferable to all.

But, said I, you have various occupations. One kind of stuff or one fashion is not equally suitable to every employment. This must produce a variety among you, as it does among us.

It does so. We find that our tools must vary with our designs. If the task requires a peculiar dress, we assume it. But as we take it up when we enter the workshop, we of course, lay it aside when we change the scene. It is not to be imagined that we wear the same garb at all times. No man enters society laden with the implements of his art. He does not visit the council hall or the theatre with his spade upon his shoulder. As little does he think of bringing thither the garb which he wore in the field. There are no such peculiarities of attitude or gesture among us, that the vesture that has proved most convenient to one in walking or sitting, should be found unsuitable to others. Do the differences of this kind prevalent among you, conform to these rules? Since every one has his stated employment, no doubt each one has a dress peculiar to himself or to those of his own profession.

No. I cannot say that among us this principle has any extensive influence. The chief difference consists in degrees of expensiveness. By inspecting the garb of a passenger, we discover not so much the trade that he pursues, as the amount of his property. Few labour whose wealth allows them to disperse with it. The garb of each is far from varying with the hours of the day. He need only conform to the changes of the seasons, and model his appearance by the laws of ostentation, in public, and by those of ease in the intervals of solitude. These principles are common to both sexes. Small is the portion of morality or taste, that is displayed by either, but in this, as in most other cases, the conduct of the females is the least faulty. But of all infractions of decorum, we should deem the assuming of the dress of one sex by those of the other, as the most flagrant. It so rarely happens, that I do not remember to have witnessed a single metamorphosis, except perhaps on the stage, and even there a female cannot evince a more egregious negligence of reputation than by personating a man.

All this, replied my friend, is so strange as to be almost

incredible. Why beings of the same nature, inhabiting the same spot, and accessible to the same influences, should exhibit such preposterous differences is wonderful. It is not possible that these modes should be equally commodious or graceful. Custom may account for the continuance, but not for the origin of manners.

The wonder that you express, said I, is in its turn a subject of surprise to me. What you now say, induces me to expect that among you, women and men are more similarly treated than elsewhere. But this to me, is so singular a spectacle, that I long to hear it more minutely described by you, and to witness it myself.

If you remain long enough among us you will not want the opportunity. I hope you will find that every one receives that portion which is due to him, and since a diversity of sex cannot possibly make any essential difference in the claims and duties of reasonable beings, this difference will never be found. But you call upon me for descriptions. With what hues shall I delineate the scene? I have exhibited as distinctly as possible the equity that governs us. Its maxims are of various application. They regulate our conduct, not only to each other, but to the tribes of insects and birds. Every thing is to be treated as capable of happiness itself, or as instrumental to the happiness of others.

But since the sexual differences is something, said I, and since you are not guilty of the error of treating different things as if they were the same, doubtless in your conduct towards each other, the consideration of sex is of some weight.

Undoubtedly. A species of conduct is incumbent upon men and women towards each other on certain occasions, that cannot take place between man and man; or between women and women. I may properly supply my son with a razor to remove superfluous hairs from his chin, but I may with no less propriety forbear to furnish my daughter with this impliment, because nature has denied her a beard; but all this is so evident that I cannot but indulge a smile at the formality with which you state it.

But, said I, it is the nature and extent of this difference of treatment that I want to know.

Be explicit my good friend. Do you want a physiological dissertation on this subject or not? If you do, excuse me from performing the task, I am unequal to it.

No. But I will try to explain myself, what for example is the difference which takes place in the education of the two sexes?

There is no possible ground for difference. Nourishment is imparted and received in the same way. Their organs of digestion and secretion are the same. There is one diet, one regimen, one mode and degree of exercise, best adapted to unfold the powers of the human body, and maintain them for the longest time in full vigour. One individual may be affected by some casualty or disease, so as to claim to be treated in a manner different from another individual, but this difference is not necessarily connected with sex. Neither sex is exempt from injury, contracted through their own ignorance, or that of others. Doubtless the sound woman and the sick man it would be madness to subject to the same tasks, or the same regimen. But this is no less true if both be of the same sex. Diseases, on whichsoever they fall, are curable by the same means.

Human beings in their infancy, continued my friend, require the same tendance and instruction: but does one sex require more or less, or a different sort of tendance or instruction than the other? Certainly not. If by any fatal delusion, one sex should imagine its interest to consist in the ill treatment of the other, time would soon detect their mistake. For how is the species to be continued? How is a woman, for example, to obtain a sound body, and impart it to her offspring, but, among other sources, from the perfect constitution of both her parents? But it is needless to argue on a supposition so incredible as that mankind can be benefitted by injustice and oppression.

Would we render the limbs supple, vigorous and active? And are there two modes equally efficacious of attaining this end? Must we suppose that one sex will find this end of less value than the other, or the means suitable to its attainment different? It cannot be supposed.

We are born with faculties that enable us to impart and receive happiness. There is one species of discipline, better adapted than any other to open and improve those faculties. This mode is to be practised. All are to be furnished with the means of instruction, whether these consist in the direct commerce of the senses with the material universe, or in intercourse with other intelligent beings. It is requisite to know the reasonings, actions and opinions of others, if we seek the improvement of our own understanding. For this end we must see them, and talk with them if present, or if distant or dead, we must consult these memorials which have been contrived by themselves or others. These are simple and intelligible maxims proper to regulate our treatment of rational beings. The only circumstance to which we are bound to attend is that the subjects of instruction be rational. If any one observe that the consideration of sex is of some moment, how must his remark be understood. Would he insinuate that because my sex is different from yours, one of us only can be treated as rational, or that though reason be a property of both, one of us possesses less of it than the other. I am not born among a people who can countenance so monstrous a doctrine.

No two persons are entitled in the strictest sense, to the same treatment, because no two can be precisely alike. All the possibilities and shades of difference, no human capacity can estimate. Observation will point out some of the more considerable sources of variety. Man is a progressive being, he is wise in proportion to the number of his ideas, and to the accuracy with which he compares and arranges them. These ideas are received through the inlets of his senses. They must be successively received. The objects which suggest them, must be present. There must be time for observation. Hence the difference is, in some degree, uniform between the old and the young. Between those, the sphere of whose observation has been limited, and those whose circle is extensive. Such causes as these of difference are no less incident to one sex than to the other. The career of both commences in childhood and ignorance. How far and how swiftly they may proceed before their steps are arrested by disease, or death, is to be inferred from a knowledge of their circumstances: such as betide them simply as individuals.

It would, perhaps, be unreasonable to affirm that the circumstance of sex affects in no degree the train of ideas in the mind. It is not possible that any circumstance, however trivial, should be totally without mental influence; but we may safely affirm that this circumstance is indeed trivial, and its consequences, therefore, unimportant. It is inferior to most other incidents of human existence, and to those which are necessarily incident to both sexes. He that resides among hills, is a different mortal from him that dwells on a plain. Subterranean darkness, or the seclusion of a valley, suggest ideas of a kind different from those that occur to us on the airy verge of a promontory, and in the neighbourhood of roaring waters. The influence on my character which flows from my age, from the number and quality of my associates, from the nature of my dwelling place, as sultry or cold, fertile or barren, level or diversified, the art that I cultivate, the extent or frequency of my excursions cannot be of small moment. In comparison with this, the qualities which are to be ascribed to my sex are unworthy of being mentioned. No doubt my character is in some degree tinged by it, but the tinge is inexpressibly small.

You give me leave to conclude then, said I, that the same method of education is pursued with regard to both sexes?

Certainly, returned my philosopher. Men possess powers that may be drawn forth and improved by exercise and discipline. Let them be so, says our system. It contents itself with prescribing certain general rules to all that bear the appellation of human. It permits all to refresh and invigorate their frames by frequenting the purest streams and the pleasantest fields, and by practising those gestures and evolutions that tend to make us robust and agile. It admits the young to the assemblies of their elders, and exhorts the elder to instruct the young. It multiplies the avenues, and facilitates the access to knowledge. Conversations, books, instruments, specimens of the productions of art and nature, haunts of meditation, and public halls, liberal propensities and leisure, it is the genius of our system to create, multiply, and place within the reach of all. It is far from creation, and debasing its views, by distinguishing those who dwell on the shore from those that inhabit the hills; the beings whom a cold temperature has bleached, from those that are embrowned by an hot.

But different persons, said I, have different employments. Skill cannot be obtained in them without a regular course of instruction. Each sex has, I doubt not, paths of its own into which the others must not intrude. Hence must arise a difference in their education.

Who has taught you, replied he, that each sex must have

peculiar employments? Your doubts and your conjectures are equally amazing. One would imagine that among you, one sex had more arms, or legs, or senses than the other. Among us there is no such inequality. The principles that direct us in the choice of occupations are common to all.

Pray tell me, said I, what these principles are.

They are abundantly obvious. There are some tasks which are equally incumbent upon all. These demand no more skill and strength than is possessed by all. Men must provide themselves by their own efforts with food, clothing and shelter. As long as they live together there is a duty obliging them to join their skill and their exertions for the common benefit. A certain portion of labour will supply the needs of all. This portion then must be divided among all. Each one must acquire and exert the skill which this portion requires. But this skill and this strength are found by experience to be moderate and easily attained. To plant maize, to construct an arch, to weave a garment, are no such arduous employments but that all who have emerged from the infirmity and ignorance of childhood, may contribute their efforts to the performance.

But besides occupations which are thus of immediate and universal utility, there is an infinite variety of others. The most exquisite of all calamities, results from a vacant mind and unoccupied limbs. The highest pleasure demands the ceaseless activity of both. To enjoy this pleasure it is requisite to find some other occupation of our time, beside those which are enjoined by the physical necessities of our nature. Among these there is ample room for choice. The motives that may influence us in this choice, are endless. I shall not undertake to enumerate them. You can be at no loss to conceive them without my assistance: but whether they be solitary or social, whether speech or books, or observation, or experiment be the medium of instruction, there can be nothing in the distinction of sex to influence our determinations, or this influence is so inconsiderable as not to be worth mention.

What, cried I, are all obliged to partake of all the labours of tilling the ground, without distinction of rank and sex?

Certainly. There are none that fail to consume some portion of the product of the ground. To exempt any from a share in the cultivation, would be an inexpiable injustice, both to those who are exempted and those who are not exempted. The exercise is cheerful and wholesome. Its purpose is just and necessary. Who shall dare to deny me a part in it? But we know full well that the task, which, if divided among many, is easy and salubrious, is converted into painful and unwholesome drudgery, by being confined to a sex, what phrenzy must that be which should prompt us to introduce a change in this respect? I cannot even imagine so great a perversion of the understanding. Common madness is unequal to so monstrous a conception. We must first not only cease to be reasonable, but cease to be men. Even that supposition is insufficient, for into what class of animals must we sink, before this injustice could be realized? Among beasts there are none who do not owe their accommodations to their own exertions.

Food is no less requisite to one sex than to the other. As the necessity of food, so the duty of providing it is common. But the reason why I am to share in the labour, is not merely because I am to share in the fruits. I am a being guided by reason and susceptible of happiness. So are other men. It is therefore a privilege that I cannot relinquish, to promote and contemplate the happiness of others. After the cravings of necessity are satisfied, it remains for me, by a new application of my powers, to enlarge the pleasures of existence. The inlets to this pleasure are numberless. What can prompt us to take from any the power of choosing among these, or to incapacitate him from choosing with judgment. The greater the number of those who are employed in administering to pleasure, the greater will be the product. Since both sexes partake of this capacity, what possible reasons can there be for limiting or precluding the efforts of either?

What I conceive to be unjust, may yet be otherwise; but my actions will conform to my opinions. If you would alter the former, you must previously introduce a change into the latter. I know the opinions of my countrymen. The tenor of their actions will conform to their notions of right. Can the time ever come, will the power ever arise, that shall teach them to endure the oppression of injustice themselves, or inflict it upon others? No.

But in my opinion, said I, the frame of women is too

delicate, their limbs too minute for rough and toilsome occupations. I would rather confine them to employments more congenial to the female elements of softness and beauty.

You would rather, would you? I will suppose you sincere, and inquire how you would expect to obtain their consent to your scheme.

The sentiments, said I, of a single individual, would avail nothing. But if all the males should agree to prescribe their employments to women—

What then? interrupted my friend. There are but two methods of effecting this end—by force or by persuasion. With respect to force we cannot suppose human beings capable of it, for any moral purpose; but supposing them capable, we would scarcely resort to force, while our opponents are equal in number, strength and skill to ourselves. The efficacy of persuasion is equally chimerical. That frailty of mind which should make a part of mankind willing to take upon themselves a double portion of the labour, and to convert what is pleasurable exercise to all, into a source of pain and misery to a few. But these are vain speculations, let us dismiss them from our notice.

Willingly, said I, we will dismiss these topics for the sake of one more important.

I presume then, said I, there is such a thing as marriage among you.

I do not understand the term.

I use it to express that relation which subsists between two human beings in consequence of difference of sex.

You puzzle me exceedingly, returned he. You question me as to the existence of that concerning which it is impossible for you to be ignorant. You cannot at this age be a stranger to the origin of human existence.

When I had gotten thus far in my narrative, I paused. Mrs. Carter still continued to favour me with her attention. On observing my silence she desired me to proceed.

I presume, said she, your supernatural conductor allowed you to finish the conversation. To snatch you away just now, in the very midst of your subject, would be doing you and me likewise a very unacceptable office. I beseech you go on with the discourse.

It may not be proper, answered I. This is a topic on which, strange to tell, we cannot discourse in the same terms before every audience. The remainder of our conversation decorum would not perhaps forbid you to read, but it prohibits you from hearing. If you wish it, I will give you the substance of the information I collected on this topic in writing.

What is improper to be said in my hearing, said the lady, it should seem was no less improper to be knowingly addressed to me by the pen.

Then, said I, you do not assent to my offer.

Nay, I do not refuse my assent. I merely object to the distinction, that you have raised. There are many things improper to be uttered, or written, or to be read, or listened to, but the impropriety methinks must adhere to the sentiments themselves, and not result from the condition of the author or his audience.

Are these your real sentiments?

Without doubt. But they appear not to be yours. However write what you please, I promise you to read it, and to inform you of my opinion respecting it. Your scheme, I suspect, will not be what is commonly called marriage, but something in your opinion, better. This footing is a dubious one. Take care, it is difficult to touch without overstepping the verge.

Your caution is reasonable. I believe silence will be the safest. You will excuse me therefore from taking up the pen on this occasion. The ground you say, and I believe, is perilous. It will be most prudent to avoid it.

As you please, but remember that though I may not approve of what you write, your silence I shall approve still less. If it be false, it will enable me at least to know you, and I shall thereby obtain an opportunity of correcting your mistakes. Neither of these purposes are trivial. Are you not aware that no future declaration of yours will be more unfavourable than what you have just said, that silence will be most safe. You are afraid no doubt, of shocking too greatly my prejudices; but you err. I am certainly prepossessed in favour of the system of marriage, but the strength of this prepossession will appear only in the ardour of my compassion for contrary opinions, and the eagerness of my endeavours to remove them.

You would condescend then, said I, to reason on the subject, as if it were possible that marriage was an erroneous institution; as if it were possible that any one could seriously maintain it to be, without entitling himself to the imputation of the lowest profligacy. Most women would think that the opponent of marriage, either assumed the character for the most odious and selfish purposes, and could therefore only deserve to be treated as an assassin: to be detested and shunned, or if he were sincere in his monstrous faith, that all efforts to correct his mistakes would avail nothing with respect to the patient, but might endanger the physician by exposing her to the illusions of sophistry or the contagion of passion.

I am not one of these, said the lady. The lowest stupidity only can seek its safety in shutting its ears. We may call that sophistry, which having previously heard, it fails to produce conviction. Yet sophistry perhaps implies not merely fallacious reasoning, but a fallaciousness of which the reasoner himself is apprised. If so, few charges ought to be made with more caution. But nothing can exceed the weakness that prevents us from attending to what is going to be urged against our opinions, merely from the persuasion that what is adverse to our preconceptions must be false. Yet there are examples of this folly among our acquaintance. You are wrong, said I lately to one of these, if you will suffer me, I will convince you of your error. You may save yourself the trouble, she answered. You may torment me with doubts, but why, when I see the truth clearly already, should I risque the involving of it in obscurity? I repeat, I am not of this class. Force is to be resisted by force, or eluded by flight: but he that argues, whatever be his motives, should be encountered with argument. He cannot commit a greater error than to urge topics, the insufficiency of which is known to himself. To demonstrate this error is as worthy of truth as any other province. To sophistry, in any sense of the term, the proper antidote is argument. Give me leave to take so much interest in your welfare, as to desire to see your errors corrected, and to contribute what is in my power to that end. If I know myself so well as sometimes to listen to others in the hope of profiting by their superior knowledge or sagacity, permit me likewise to be just to myself in other respects, and to believe myself capable sometimes of pointing out his mistakes to another.

You seem, said I, to think it certain that we differ in opinion upon this topic.

No. I merely suspect that we do. A class of reasoners has lately arisen, who aim at the deepest foundation of civil society. Their addresses to the understanding have been urged with no despicable skill. But this was insufficient, it was necessary to subdue our incredulity, as to the effects of their new maxims, by exhibiting those effects in detail, and winning our assent to their truth by engrossing the fancy and charming the affections. The journey that you have lately made, I merely regard as an excursion into their visionary world. I can trace the argument of the parts which you have unfolded, with those which are yet to come, and can pretty well conjecture of what hues, and lines, and figures, the remainder of the picture is intended to consist.

Then, said I, the task that I enjoined on myself is superfluous. You are apprised of all that I mean to say on the topic of marriage, and have already laid in an ample stock of disapprobation for my service.

I frankly confess that I expect not to approve the matter of your narrative, however pleased I may be with the manner. Nevertheless I wish you to execute your first design, that I may be able to unveil the fallacy of your opinions, and rescue one whom I have no reason to disrespect, from specious but fatal illusions.

Your purpose is kind. It entitles you at least to my thanks. Yet to say truth, I did not at first despair of your confidence with me in some of my opinions. I imagined that some of the evils of marriage had not escaped you. I recollect that during our last conversation, you arraigned with great earnestness the injustice of condemning women to obey the will, and depend upon the bounty of father or husband.

Come, come, interrupted the lady, with a severer aspect, if you mean to preserve my good opinion, you must tread on this ground with more caution. Remember the atrociousness of the charge you would insinuate. What! Because a just indignation at the iniquities that are hourly committed on one half of the human species rises in my heart, because I vindicate the plainest dictates of justice, and am willing to rescue so large a portion of humankind, from so destructive a bondage: a bondage not only of the hands, but of the understanding; which divests them of all those energies which distinguish men from the basest animals, destroys all perception of moral rectitude, and reduces its subjects to so calamitous a state, that they adore the tyranny that rears its crest over them, and kiss the hand that loads them with ignominy! When I demand an equality of conditions among beings that equally partake of the same divine reason, would you rashly infer that I was an enemy to the institution of marriage itself? Where shall we look for human beings who surpass all others in depravity and wretchedness? Are they not to be found in the haunts of female licentiousness. If their vice admits of a darker hue, it would receive it from the circumstance of their being dissolute by theory; of their modelling voluptuousness into a speculative system. Yet this is the charge you would make upon me. You would brand me as an enemy to marriage, not in the sense that a vestal, or widow, or chaste, but deserted maid is an enemy; not even in that sense in which the abandoned victims of poverty and temptation are enemies, but in the sense of that detestable philosophy which scoffs at the matrimonial institution itself, which denies all its pretensions to sanctity, which consigns us to the guidance of a sensual impulse, and treats as phantastic or chimerical, the sacred charities of husband, son, and brother. Beware. Imputations of this kind are more fatal in the consequences than you may be able to conceive. They cannot be indifferent to me. In drawing such inferences, you would hardly be justified by the most disinterested intentions.

Such inferences, my dear Madam, it is far from my intention to draw. I cannot but think your alarms unnecessary. If I am an enemy to marriage far be it from me to be the champion of sensuality. I know the sacredness of this word in the opinions of mankind; I know how liable to be misunderstood are the efforts of him who should labour to explode it. But still, is it not possible to define with so much perspicuity, and distinguish with so much accuracy as to preclude all possibility of mistake? I believe this possible. I deem it easy to justify the insinuation that you yourself are desirous of subverting the marriage state.

Proceed, said the lady. Men are at liberty to annex to words what meaning they think proper. What should hinder you, if you so please, from saying that snow is of the deepest black? Words are arbitrary. The idea that others annex to the word black, you are at liberty to transfer to the word white. But in the use of this privilege you must make your account in not being understood, and in reversing all the purposes of language.

Well, said I, that is yet to appear. Meanwhile, I pray you, what are *your* objections to the present system?

My objections are weighty ones. I disapprove of it, in the first place, because it renders the female a slave to the man. It enjoins and enforces submission on her part to the will of her husband. It includes a promise of implicit obedience and unalterable affection. Secondly, it leaves the woman destitute of property. Whatever she previously possesses, belongs absolutely to the man.

This representation seems not to be a faithful one, said I. Marriage leaves the wife without property, you say.

How comes it then that she is able to subsist? You will answer, perhaps, that her sole dependence is placed upon the bounty of her husband. But this is surely an error. It is by virtue of express laws that all property subsists. But the same laws sanction the title of a wife to a subsistence proportioned to the estate of her husband. But if law were silent, custom would enforce this claim. The husband is in reality nothing but a steward. He is bound to make provision for his wife, proportionately to the extent of his own revenue. This is a practical truth, of which every woman is sensible. It is this that renders the riches of an husband a consideration of so much moment in the eye of a prudent woman. To select a wealthy partner is universally considered as the certain means of enriching ourselves, not less when the object of our choice is an husband than when it is a wife.

Notwithstanding all this, said the lady, you will not pretend to affirm that marriage renders the property common.

May I not truly assert, rejoined I, that the wife is legally entitled to her maintenance?

Yes, she is entitled to food, raiment, and shelter, if her husband can supply them. Suppose a man in possession of five thousand pounds a year: from this the wife is entitled to maintenance: but how shall the remainder be administered? Is not the power of the husband, over this, absolute? Cannot he reduce himself to poverty to-morrow? She may claim a certain portion of what she has, but he may, at his own pleasure, divest himself of all that he has. He may expend it on what purposes he pleases. It is his own, and, for the use of it, he is responsible to no tribunal; but in reality, this pompous claim of his wife amounts, in most cases, to nothing. It is the discretion of the husband that must decide, as to the kind and quantity of that provision. He may be niggardly or prodigal, according to the suggestions of his own caprice. He may hasten to poverty himself, or he may live, and compel his partner to live, in the midst of wealth as if he were labouring under extreme indigence. In neither case has the wife any remedy.

But recollect, my good friend, the husband is commonly the original proprietor. Has the wife a just claim to that which, before marriage, belonged to her spouse?

Certainly not. Nor is it less true that the husband has no just claim to that which, previously to marriage, belonged to the wife. If property were, in all respects, justly administered, if patrimonies were equally divided among offspring, and if the various avenues that lead to the possession of property were equally accessible to both sexes, it would be found as frequently and extensively vested in one son as in the other. Marriage is productive of no consequences which justify the transfer of what either previously possessed to the other. The idea of common property is absurd and pernicious; but even this is better than poverty and dependence to which the present system subjects the female.

But, said I, it is not to be forgotten that the household is common. One dwelling, one table, one set of servants

73

may justly be sustained by a single fund. This fund may be managed by common consent. No particle of expense may accrue without the concurrence of both parties, but if there be a difference of opinion, some one must ultimately decide. Why should not this be the husband? You will say that this would be unjust. I answer that, since it is necessary that power should be vested in one or the other the injustice is inevitable. An opposite procedure would not diminish it. If this necessary power of deciding in cases of disagreement were lodged in the wife, the injustice would remain.

But a common fund and a common dwelling is superfluous. Why is marriage to condemn two human beings to dwell under the same roof and to eat at the same table, and to be served by the same domestics? This circumstance alone is the source of innumerable ills. Familiarity is the sure destroyer of reverence. All the bickerings and dissentions of a married life flow from no other source than that of too frequent communication. How difficult is it to introduce harmony of sentiment, even on topics of importance, between two persons? But this difficulty is increased in proportion to the number and frequency, and the connection with our private and personal deportment of these topics.

If two persons are condemned to cohabitation, there must doubtless be mutual accommodation. But let us understand this term. No one can sacrifice his opinions. What is incumbent upon him, in certain cases, is only to forbear doing what he esteems to be right. Now that situation is most eligible in which we are at liberty to conform to the dictates of our judgment. Situations of a different kind will frequently occur in human life. Many of them exist without any necessity. Such, in its present state, is matrimony.

Since an exact agreement of opinions is impossible, and since the intimate and constant intercourse of a married life requires either that the parties should agree in their opinions, or that one should forego his own resolutions, what is the consequence? Controversies will incessantly arise, and must be decided. If argument be insufficient, recourse must be had to legal authority, to brute force, or servile artifices, or to that superstition that has bound itself by a promise to obey. These might be endured if they were the necessary attendants of marriage; but they are spurious additions. Marriage is a sacred institution, but it would argue the most pitiful stupidity to imagine that all those circumstances which accident and custom have annexed to it are likewise sacred. Marriage is sacred, but iniquitous laws, by making it a compact of slavery, by imposing impracticable conditions and extorting impious promises have, in most countries, converted it into something flagitious and hateful.

But the marriage promises, said I, amount to this, that the parties shall love each other till death. Would you impose no restraint on wayward inclinations? Shall this contract subsist no longer than suits the wishes of either party? Would you grant, supposing you exalted into a law-giver, an unlimited power of divorces?

Without the least doubt. What shadow of justice is there in restraining mankind in this particular. My liberty is precious, but of all the ways in which my liberty can be infringed, and my actions be subjected to force, heaven deliver me from this species of constraint. It is impossible to do justice to my feelings on this occasion. Offer me any alternative, condemn me to the workshop of an Egyptian task-master, imprison me in chains of darkness, tear me into pieces, subject me to the endless repetition of toil and stripes and contumelies, but allow me, I beseech you, the liberty, at least, of conjugal choice. If you prohibit my intercourse with one on whom my heart dotes, I shall not repine, the injury is inexpressibly trivial. There is scarcely an inconvenience that will be worth enduring for the sake of this prohibited good. My resources must be few, indeed, if they do not afford me consolation under this injustice. But if you subject me to the controul and the nauseous caresses of one whom I hate, or despise, you indeed inflict a calamity which nothing can compensate. There is no form which your injustice can assume more detestable and ugly than this.

According to present modes, the servitude of wives is the most entire and unremitting. She lays aside her fetters not for a moment. There is not an action, however minute, in which her tyrant does not assume the power of prescribing. His eyes are eternally upon her. There is no period, however short, in which she is exempt from his cognizance; no recess, however sacred or mysterious, into which he does not intrude. She cannot cherish the friendship of a human being without his consent. She cannot dispense a charitable farthing without his connivance. The beings who owe their existence to her, are fashioned by his sole and despotic will. All their dignity and happiness is lodged in the hands that superintend their education and prescribe their conduct during the important periods of infancy and youth. But how they shall exist, what shall be taught, and what shall be withholden from them, what precepts they shall hear, and what examples they shall contemplate, it is his province to decide.

An husband is proposed to me. I ruminate on these facts. I ponder on this great question. Shall I retain my liberty or not? Perhaps the evils of my present situation, the pressure of poverty, the misjudging rule of a father, or the rare qualities of him who is proposed to me, the advantages of change of place or increase of fortune, may outweigh the evils of this state. Perhaps I rely on the wisdom of my partner. I am assured that he will, in all cases, trust to nothing but the force of reason; that his arguments will always convince, or his candour be accessible to conviction; that he will never make his appeal to personal or legal coersion, but allow me the dominion of my own conduct when he cannot persuade me to compliance with his wishes. These considerations may induce me to embrace the offer.

If I am not deceived; if no inauspicious revolution take place in his character; if circumstances undergo no material alteration; if I continue to love and to confide as at the first, it is well. I cannot object to a perpetual alliance, provided it be voluntary. There is nothing, in a choice of this kind, that shall necessarily cause it to expire. This alliance will be durable in proportion to the wisdom with which it was formed, and the foresight that was exerted.

But if a change take place, if I were deceived, and find insolence and peevishness, rigour and command, where I expected nothing but sweet equality and unalterable complaisance; or if the character be changed, if time introduce new modes of thinking and new systems of action to which my understanding refuses to assimilate, what is the consequence? Shall I not revoke my choice?

The hardships of constraint in this respect are peculiarly severe upon the female. Her's is the task of submission. In every case of disagreement it is she that must yield. The man still retains, in a great degree, his independence. In the choice of his abode, his occupations, his associates, his tasks and his pleasures, he is guided by his own judgment. The conduct of his wife, the treatment of her offspring, and the administration of her property are consigned to him. All the evils of constraint are aggravated by the present system. But if the system were reformed, if the duties of marriage extended to nothing but occasional interviews and personal fidelity, if each retained power over their own actions in all cases not immediately connected with the sensual intercourse, the obligation to maintain this intercourse, after preference had ceased, would be eminently evil. Less so, indeed, than in the present state of marriage, but still it would be fertile in misery. Have you any objections to this conclusion?

I cannot say that I have many. You know what is commonly urged in questions of this kind. Men, in civil society are, in most cases, subjected to a choice of evils. That which is injurious to one, or a few individuals, may yet be beneficial to the whole. In an estimate, sufficiently comprehensive, the good may overweigh the ill. You have drawn a forcible picture of the inconveniences attending the prohibition of divorces. Perhaps if entire liberty in this respect were granted, the effects might constitute a scene unspeakably more disastrous than any thing hitherto conceived.

As how, I pray you?

Men endeavour to adhere with a good grace to a contract which they cannot infringe. That which is commonly termed love is a vagrant and wayward principle. It pretends to spurn at those bounds which decorum and necessity prescribe to it, and yet, at the same time, is tamely and rigidly observant of those bounds. This passion commonly betides us when we have previously reasoned ourselves into the belief of the propriety of entertaining it. It seldom visits us but at the sober invitation of our judgment. It speedily takes its leave when its presence becomes uneasy, and its gratification ineligible or impossible. Youth and beauty, it is said, have a tendency to excite this passion, but suppose those qualities are discovered in a sister, what becomes of this tendency? Suppose the possession to be already a wife. If chance place us near an object of uncommon loveliness and we are impressed with a notion that she is single and dis-engaged, our hearts may be in some danger. But suppose better information has precluded this mistake, or that it is immediately rectified, the danger in most cases, is at an end. I am married and have no power to dissolve the contract. Will this consideration have no power over my sensations in the presence of a stranger? If care, accomplishments, and inimitable loveliness attract my notice, after my lot is decided, and chained me to one, with whom the comparison is disadvantageous, I may indulge a faint wish that my destiny had otherwise decreed; a momentary sigh at the irrevocableness of my choice, but my regrets will instantly vanish. Recollecting that my fate is indeed decided, and my lot truly irrevocable, I become cheerful and calm.

It is true that harmony cannot be expected to subsist for ever and in every minute instance between two persons, but how far will the consciousness that the ill is without remedy, and the condition of affairs unchangeable, tend to foster affection and generate mutual compliance. Human beings are distinguished by nothing more than by a propensity to imitation. They contract affection and resemblance with those persons or objects that are placed near them. The force of habit, in this respect, is admirable. Even inanimate objects become, through the influence of this principle, necessary to our happiness. They that are constant companions fail not to become, in most respects, alike, and to be linked together by the perception of this likeness. Their modes of acting and thinking might, at first, have jarred, but these modes are not in their own nature, immutable. The benefits of concurrence, the inconveniences of opposition, and the opportunities of comparing and weighing the grounds of their differences cannot be supposed to be without some tendency to produce resemblance and sympathy.

This is plausible, said the lady, but what is your aim in stating these remarks? Do you mean by them to extenuate the evils that arise from restraining divorces?

If they contribute to that end, answered I, it is proper to urge them. They promote a good purpose. Your picture was so terrible that I am willing to employ any expedient for softening its hues.

If it were just, you ought to have admitted its justice. We see the causes of these evils. They admit of an obvious remedy. A change in the opinions of a nation is all that is requisite for this end. But let us examine your pleas, or rather, instead of reasoning on the subject, let us turn our eyes on the world and its scenes, and mark the effect of this spirit by which human beings are prompted to adopt the opinions, and dote upon the presence of those whom accident has placed beside them. It would be absurd to deny all influence to habit and all force to reflections upon the incurableness of the evil, but what is the effect they produce? In numberless cases the married life is a scene of perpetual contention and strife. A transient observer frequently perceives this, but in cases where appearances are more specious, he that has an opportunity to penetrate the veil which hangs over the domestic scene, is often disgusted with a spectacle of varied and exquisite misery. Nothing is to be found but a disgusting train of mean compliances, despicable artifices, pevishness, recriminations and falsehood. It is rare that fortitude and consideration are exercised by either party. Their misery is heightened by impatience and tormenting recollections, but the few whose minds are capable of fortitude, who estimate the evil at its just value, and profit by the portion of good, whatever it be, that remains to them, experience indeed, sensations less acute, and pass fewer moments of bitterness; but it is from the unhappy that patience is demanded. This virtue does not annihilate the evil that oppresses us, but lightens it. It does not destroy in us the consciousness of privileges of which we are destitute, or of joys which have taken their flight. Its office is to prevent these reflections from leading us to rage and despair; to make us look upon lost happiness without relapsing into phrenzy; to establish in our bosoms the empire of cold and solemn indifference.

If the exercise of reason and the enjoyment of liberty be valuable; if the effusions of genuine sympathy and the adherence to an unbiassed and enlightened choice, be the true element of man, what shall we think of that harmony which is the result of narrow views and that sympathy which is the offspring of constraint?

I know that love, as it is commonly understood, is an empty and capricious passion. It is a sensual attachment which, when unaccompanied with higher regards, is truly contemptible. To thwart it is often to destroy it, and sometimes, to qualify the victims of its delusions for Bedlam. In the majority of cases it is nothing but a miserable project of affectation. The languishing and sighing lover is an object to which the errors of mankind have annexed a certain degree of reverence. Misery is our title to compassion, and to men of limited capacities the most delicious potion that can be administered is pity. For the sake of this, hundreds are annually metamorphosed into lovers. It is graceful to languish with an hopeless passion; to court the music of sighs and the secrecy of groves. But it is to be hoped that these chimeras will, at length, take their leave of us.

In proportion as men become wise, their pursuits will be judiciously selected, and that which they have wisely chosen will continue for a certain period, to be the objects of their choice. Conjugal fidelity and constancy will characterize the wise. But constancy is meritorious only within certain limits. What reverence is due to groundless and obstinate attachments? It becomes me to make the best choice that circumstances will admit, but human affairs will never be reduced to that state in which the decisions of the wisest man will be immutable. Allowance must be made for inevitable changes of situation, and for the nature of man, which is essentially progressive: That is evil which hinders him from conforming to these changes, and restrains him from the exercise of his judgment.

Let it be admitted that love is easily extinguished by reflection. Does it follow that he ought to be controuled in the choice of his companion? Your observations imply, that he that is now married to one woman, would attach himself to another, if the law did not interpose. Where are the benefits of interposition? Does it increase the happiness of him that is affected by it? Will its succour be invoked by his present consort? That a man continues to associate with me contrary to his judgment and inclination is no subject of congratulation. If law or force obliged him to endure my society, it does not compel him to feign esteem, or dissemble hatred or indifference. If the heart of my husband be estranged from me, I may possibly regard it as an evil. If in consequence of this estrangement, we separate our persons and interests, this is a desirable consequence. This is the only palliation of which the evil is susceptible.

It cannot be denied that certain inconveniences result from the disunion of a married pair, according to the present system. You have justly observed that men are reduced, in most cases, to a choice of evils. Some evils are unavoidable. Others are gratuitous and wantonly incurred. The chief evils flowing from the dissolution of marriage, are incident to the female. This happens in consequence of the iniquitous and partial treatment to which women in general are subjected. If marriage were freed from all spurious obligations, the inconveniences, attending the dissolution of it, would be reduced to nothing.

What think you, said I, of the duty we owe to our children. Is not their happiness materially affected by this species of liberty?

I cannot perceive how. I would, however, be rightly understood. I confess that, according to the present system, it would, and hence arises a new objection to this system. The children suffer, but do their sufferings, even in the present state of things, outweigh the evils resulting from the impossibility of separation? The evil that the parents endure, and the evils accruing to the offspring themselves?

If children stand in need of the guidance and protection of their elders, and particularly of their parents, it ought to be granted. The parental relation continues notwithstanding a divorce. Though they have ceased to be husband and wife to each other, they have not ceased to be father and mother to me. My claims on them are the same, and as forcible as ever. The ties by which they are bound to me, are not diminished by this event. My claim for subsistence is made upon their property. But this accident does not annihilate their property. If it impoverish one, the other is proportionably enriched. There is the same inclination and power to answer my claim: The judgment that consulted for my happiness and decided for me, before their separation, is no whit altered or lessened. On the contrary, it is most likely to be improved. When relieved from the task of tormenting each other, and no longer exposed to bickerings and disappointment, they become better qualified for any disinterested or arduous office.

But what effects, said I, may be expected from the removal of this restraint, upon the morals of the people? It seems to open a door to licentiousness and profligacy. If marriages can be dissolved and contracted at pleasure, will not every one deliver himself up to the impulse of a lawless appetite? Would not changes be incessant? All chastity of mind perhaps, would perish. A general corruption of manners would ensue, and this vice would pave the way for the admission of a thousand others, till the whole nation were sunk into a state of the lowest degeneracy.

Pray thee, cried the lady, leave this topic of declamation to the school boys—Liberty, in this respect, would eminently conduce to the happiness of mankind. A partial reformation would be insufficient. Set marriage on a right basis, and the pest that has hitherto made itself an inmate of every house, and ravaged every man's peace, will be exterminated. The servitude that has debased one half, and the tyranny that has depraved the other half of the human species will be at an end.

And with all those objections to the present regulations on this subject, you will still maintain that you are an advocate of marriage?

Undoubtedly I retain the term, and am justified by common usage in retaining it. No one imagines that the forms which law or custom, in a particular age or nation, may happen to annex to marriage are essential to it, if lawgivers should enlarge the privilege of divorce, and new modify the rights of property, as they are affected by marriage. Should they ordain that henceforth the husband should vow obedience to the wife, in place of the former vow which the wife made to the husband, or entirely prohibit promises of any kind; should they expunge from the catalogue of conjugal duties that which confines them to the same dwelling, who would imagine that the institution itself were subverted? In the east, conjugal servitude has ever been more absolute than with us, and polygamy legally established. Yet, who will affirm that marriage is unknown in the east. Every one knows that regulations respecting property, domestic government, and the causes of divorce are incident to this state, and do not constitute its essence.

I shall assent, said I, to the truth of this statement. Perhaps I may be disposed to adventure a few steps further than you. It appears to me that marriage has no other criterion than custom. This term is descriptive of that mode of sexual intercourse, whatever it may be, which custom or law has established in any country. All the modifications of this intercourse that have ever existed, or can be supposed to exist, are so many species included in the general term. The question that we have been discussing is no other than this: what species of marriage is most agreeable to justice—Or, in other words, what are the principles that ought to regulate the sexual intercourse? It is not likely that any portion of mankind have reduced these principles to practice. Hence arises a second question of the highest moment: what conduct is incumbent upon me, when the species of marriage established among my countrymen, does not conform to my notions of duty.

That indeed, returned she, is going further than I am willing to accompany you. There are many conceivable modes of sexual intercourse on which I cannot bestow the appellation of marriage. There is something which inseparably belongs to it. It is not unallowable to call by this name a state which comprehends, together with these ingredients, any number of appendages. But to call a state which wants these ingredients marriage, appears to me a perversion of language.

I pry'thee, said I, what are these ingredients? You have largely expatiated on the non-essentials of matrimony: Be good enough to say what truly belongs to this state?

Willingly, answered she. Marriage is an union founded on free and mutual consent. It cannot exist without friendship. It cannot exist without personal fidelity. As soon as the union ceases to be spontaneous it ceases to be just. This is the sum. If I were to talk for months, I could add nothing to the completeness of this definition.

NOTES

Parts I and II of the text are based on *Alcuin; A Dialogue*
(New York: T. and J. Swords, 1798), while parts III and
IV are based on sections printed in William Dunlap,
*The Life of Charles Brockden Brown: together with Selections
from the Rarest of His Printed Works, from His Original
Letters, and from His Manuscripts Before Unpublished* (Philadelphia: James P. Parke, 1815), I, 71-105. The variants
for parts I and II are taken from "The Rights of Woman.
A Dialogue," which appeared in the *Weekly Magazine*
of Philadelphia (March 17-April 7, 1798), and which
abridges the Swords edition by omitting all material
from page 29, line 27 to page 35, line 27 and substituting
one summary paragraph, and by concluding the work at
the word *perverted* on page 41. This abridgment tends to
support the notion that "The Rights of Women" is, in
fact, a condensation of the text of *Alcuin*, although the
two versions were published almost simultaneously.
Texts are reduced far more frequently than they are
amplified. The variants for parts III and IV in "The
Paradise of Women," appended to the English version
of Dunlap's biography, entitled *Memoirs of Charles Brockden
Brown, the American Novelist* (London: Henry Colburn,
1822), pp. 247-308, are insignificant. In addition to the
differences specifically noted below, the following general
variants from the two main texts may be noted: "The
Rights of Women" and "The Paradise of Women" both
set off quoted material with double quotation marks; in
addition, "The Rights of Women" capitalizes the first

letter of material quoted within a sentence and uses commas instead of parentheses to set off said I, and said she. Such variants in spelling, punctuation, grammatical construction, italics, paragraphing, and in the use or arrangement of words as do not affect meaning are not noted.

VARIANTS

page 8
The name Alcuin is changed to Edwin.

page 9
References are omitted to the edicts of Carnot, a series of repressive measures instituted by the French Executive Directory in the fall of 1796 and named after Lazare Nichols Marguerite Carnot (1753-1823), a member of the French Convention and of the Committee of Public Safety, and to Peter Porcupine, alias William Cobbett (1762-1835), at that time a defender of the Federalist position.

page 12
The derogatory remarks about soldiers and barbers are omitted.

page 13
The words *nor shoemakers* are omitted.

page 20
The slur against the clergy is omitted, and the phrase is elided to read *mercenary lawyer*.

Again, a possible slur against the clergy is omitted, and the phrase reads *law or medicine*.

AFTERWORD

The publication of this edition of Alcuin; A Dialogue *has a significance quite apart from the contents of the book. As numerous scholars have pointed out, it is the first published work by Charles Brockden Brown (1771–1810), who is generally considered to be the first professional man of letters in the United States. Parts I and II were printed originally as a book in New York in 1798 and were serialized in a slightly altered and abridged version in the* Weekly Magazine *of Philadelphia, Brown's native city, from March 17 to April 7, 1798. An advertisement dated April 24, 1798 and included at the end of the New York edition indicates that the final parts of the dialogue were written and were in the publisher's hands when the first two portions of the text went to press. But these—for unknown reasons—were never published as promised. Perhaps Brown repented of his radicalism and withdrew the final sections; perhaps the death of Brown's friend, Dr. Elihu Smith, who had urged him on in the initial venture, so disheartened Brown that he could pursue the task no further on his own; or, perhaps, he was simply involved in newer projects and lost interest in his earlier efforts. Whatever the reasons, the second half, parts III and IV, was only posthumously published in 1815, embedded in William Dunlap's biography,* The Life of Charles Brockden Brown *(later abridged as* Memoirs of Charles Brockden Brown, the American Novelist *in a London edition of 1822), and has never been issued by itself. Nor has there ever been, until now, a single volume containing the entire text of all parts of* Alcuin. *Moreover, since the New York edition of the first half is extremely rare and has only once* been reprinted (*New Haven: Carl and Margaret Rollins, 1935*) most twentieth-century readers, insofar as they are acquainted with Alcuin at all, know it only as it appears, truncated, in Dunlap. Thus, this particular volume is, if not a milestone, at least a small boundary marker in American literary history in that it is, some 170 years late, the first complete edition of the first professional work by America's first professional author.

The book's wider appeal, however, grows out of its being simultaneously the first sustained and earnest argument for the rights of women to appear in this country. The issues raised between Alcuin and Mrs. Carter might well have first arisen between Eve and Adam as the angel drove them out of Eden. That Genesis neglects to record the conversation merely proves that Moses, unlike Brockden Brown, was neither radical nor Quaker. Failure to solve the problems of women permanently or even to state them definitively persists to this day and is depressing rather than surprising. For beyond the tidy realm of physiology lies a tough and weedy wilderness of cultural and metaphysical assumptions, resistant to rational analysis and difficult to uproot. Progress here is more often measured in terms of the precision with which a formulation is rendered or an historic situation analyzed than by actual alterations in the world or in human behavior. Although new and clearer formulations and a greater understanding of the past may, and indeed occasionally do, cause political, social, or cultural changes, too often even these are merely new and nicer bottles for the same sour wine.

Alcuin represents Brown's first step into this territory. And

93

his path is marked appropriately by a curious mixture of pedantry and radicalism. Both the apparent genre—the philosophic dialogue—and the various arguments and alternatives posed by the participants are grounded in traditions more or less hoary. Plato, Aristotle, Locke, Berkeley, Defoe, Mary Astell, Mary Wollstonecraft, Godwin, and a host of other well and little known philosophers and polemecists may legitimately claim Brown as their spiritual heir. Nevertheless, the rhythm of the argument, the particular points raised and rebutted, the means by which positions are attacked and defended, the constant interplay between the two characters separate the dialogue from its philosophic antecedents and establish it on a kind of middle ground between philosophy and fiction. Brown is no Plato. His duo is no Socrates and student. Even the names of the speakers testify to the range of Brown's reading and his desire to blend pedagogy with contemporaneity. Brown perhaps chose the name Alcuin, originally a scholar, philosopher, and teacher in the court of Charlemagne, to hint that many of the opinions voiced by his male figure should be considered medieval. Mrs. Carter, however, is likely a reference to Elizabeth Carter, a wellknown eighteenth-century English bluestocking, whose views would necessarily be both more modern and more radical.

Brown's purpose is didactic, his goals Horatian. But his method is exploratory. It is, as he says, an attempt to mimic conversation rather than the formal exposition which passes for dialogue in philosophic tomes. And his appeal is imaginative and emotional as much as intellectual. The arguments of Alcuin are not often particularly subtle; nor are they always pursued with great vigor. Rather, Alcuin compels attention because, between them, Mrs. Carter and the schoolmaster touch on an enormous number of issues concerning the nature and condition of women and their relationship to what used to be called the body politic.

The case that assumptions about the status of women are political as much as moral, social, or even physiological can best be made in a country and at a time when people are self-consciously aware that such assumptions are all artifices: that men act and govern on the basis of hypotheses which they themselves construct and can therefore change rather than commandments immutably engraved. Perhaps these requirements are not very limiting. Perhaps all countries and all times feel changeable to those who live in them and most historical moments are, as the saying goes, transitional. But certainly the United States was such a place in the late eighteenth century, and certainly it is such a place today. The modernity of Brown lies in his recognition that statements about the status of women and the relationship between the sexes are both, in a larger sense, political. Alternatively, the archaism of the present century lies in our continuing failure to advance beyond the point where women nod in agreement or wince with pain as either Alcuin or Mrs. Carter puts forth a theory.

Consider Mrs. Carter. She is not, in fact, a bluestocking, as Brown might easily have made her, and as a facile reading might lead us to believe. She is, instead, a proper and apparently conventional middle-class lady, a widow with a certain amount of independence but, as Brown says, with no "uncommon merit." She manages her brother's household and ministers to the comfort of his guests, most of whom seem to be men. It was

95

her job to "direct the menials, and maintain, with suitable vigilance, the empire of order and cleanliness." Most important, "she was always at home." Her life is defined in these five words. While Alcuin toils through life nursing the old ends of tallow candles and worrying about his lack of couth, Mrs. Carter stays at home in perfumed silks, surrounded by polished crystal and required only to exhibit "skill in the superintendance of a tea table, affability and modesty, promptness to inquire, and docility to listen." When Alcuin, palpitant and no doubt sweaty, turns to ask his great first question: "Pray, Madam, are you a federalist?", Mrs. Carter exhibits her sense of decorum and politesse by merely pausing with a smile. We, less hampered by company, may laugh out loud but not without some pain. We laugh at Alcuin's naivete in thinking politics a proper gambit for opening a conversation with a lady of Mrs. Carter's attributes. But we laugh, too, more painfully, at Mrs. Carter herself, who, we assume will be able only to blush and mumble, and finally, avert her eyes.

Yet this reaction is precisely the one Brown must have intended to provoke. For the joke, it turns out, is on us. As it happens, Mrs. Carter has quite a lot to say, first about why she might be expected to know nothing at all about politics and then, as her anger grows and forces her to ever more radical positions, about why she can never assent to any political philosophy at all, as she understands the alternatives to be constituted. Alcuin's assessment of Mrs. Carter, which at first seemed to be either confused or ironic, turns out to be merely accurate. Mrs. Carter is, exactly as Alcuin perceived her, a proper bourgeois lady. But Brown shows—and we, still, too often forget—that appearances do not determine intellect, that propriety is not synonymous with mindlessness, and that an outward conformity to a social code does not necessarily indicate an inner submission to it. A middle-class matron can ponder serious subjects, and her opinions on these subjects may shatter our preconceived notions of the mind that shaped them.

She begins cautiously. Why ask her if she is a federalist? Women, she says, know nothing about such matters because they have had no positive and many negative reinforcements for such knowledge. They know about ribbons and porcelain, about novels and harpsichords, and are encouraged to know little else. For such narrowness not they, but their educations and the attitudes of those around them are to blame. As Alcuin suggests, it is no reflection on the general intelligence of women that they have produced no Newton, Socrates, or Locke since "one has a better chance of becoming an astronomer by gazing at the stars through a telescope, than in eternally plying the needle, or snapping the scissars. To settle a bill of fare, to lard a pig, to compose a pudding, to carve a goose, are tasks that do not, in any remarkable degree, tend to instil the love, or facilitate the acquisition of literature and science."

In making this point, Brown has Alcuin explode the propositional sequence most commonly used, even today, to prove that nature designed women as machines miraculously fit for domestic servitude and little else. The steps in this sequence are as follows:

1. A sex which produces no Newtons is defective.
2. A sex which is defective is fit only for servility.
3. Women have produced no Newtons.
4. Therefore, women are fit only for servility.

Nurture, says Alcuin, as well as nature, must be considered if one is seriously trying to account for the triviality of most women's concerns. Thus, the first proposition is too simple to be self-evidently true. Like Virginia Woolf a century and a quarter later, Brockden Brown realizes the futility of talking about the condition of women without taking account of the environment which produces it. Only after women have rooms of their own, educations appropriate for worldly producers rather than household angels, and truly open roads away from bondage to husband, house, and children is a discussion of the accomplishments of women relative to those of men appropriate.

As the balance of the argument shifts to Mrs. Carter at this point, and as the pressure of her attack forces Alcuin's retreat, we see, however, that this initial stance was platitudinous or, at best, was based on an incomplete understanding of the factors that operate to shape a human life. Alcuin is the fossil prototype of the much denounced contemporary liberal, whose positions turn out to be more theoretical than practical. His applause, finally, is saved to endorse the private actions of individual women who, he seems to feel, ought to be made to realize that they can do more with what they already have than they seem to be doing. But, as Mrs. Carter points out, if a woman has babies and raises them, nurses the sick, remains out of the public eye, is frivolously educated and not encouraged to learn more, then it is useless or worse, cynical, to say that she has the leisure, curiosity, and moral discernment to choose the worthiest occupations. And even if an occasional woman circumvents the restrictions put upon her, this escape, far from opening new territory to the majority, is, paradoxically, used by both sexes as further proof that those who have not found the loopholes are fools who deserve their bondage.

The rationalizations—and I use the word advisedly—offered by Alcuin continue to be advanced, and as they did not console Mrs. Carter so there are some of us they do not console today. The assumptions, however true, that a desire for learning comes not from public and often corrupt institutions but from inner drive, that men practice their professions for venal and mercenary motives and that therefore these professions are not worth the respect generally accorded them, that the work traditionally done by women is more pleasant than that done by men, and that, in any case, it is a fallen world, do not destroy the link between intellectual vigor, rigorous education, and professional activity which, at its highest as well as its lowest levels, binds male to male and excludes women. Sexually segregated education, however acceptable in theory, tends generally to produce sexually segregated curricula which in turn further divide the sexes into master and slave. Woman is further brutalized when the tendencies of schools are reinforced by the conditions of marriage, when a woman's educational deficiencies are supplemented by her economic and physical bondage.

Brown's aptitude for comprehending both women's anger and the internal contradictions often involved in a particular feminist's position has been equalled, but not, I think, surpassed. The rendering of some of Mrs. Carter's more vitriolic remarks is quite brilliant:

> *The will of her husband is the criterion of all her duties. All merit is comprised in unlimited obedience. She must not expostulate or rebel. In all contests with him, she must*

hope to prevail by blandishments and tears; not by appeals to justice and addresses to reason. She will be most applauded when she smiles with most perseverence on her oppressor, and when, with the undistinguishing attachment of a dog, no caprice or cruelty shall be able to estrange her affection.

But, Mrs. Carter, it is worth noting again, is a widow. She is, to some extent, one of those exceptions previously mentioned, and, conscious of being such, she can, without apparent difficulty, denounce the generality of her sex as "thoughtless and servile creatures." Where she differs from the mass is in thinking the situation remediable.

Unfortunately, the political institutions of late eighteenth-century America, like most political institutions, far from being a source of reform, merely recapitulate and reinforce the existing social norms. The egalitarian language of those great American documents, the Declaration of Independence, the Constitution, and the Bill of Rights is mere cant—"plausible and specious maxims! but fallacious"—as far as women are concerned. Women have nothing to do with politics not only because they are educated to be apolitical, but also because politics excludes them. If culture, in some general sense, shapes personality, then it is indeed foolish to ask a woman her political beliefs, since federalist and non-federalist alike "thought as little of comprehending us in their code of liberty, as if we were pigs or sheep."

This exclusion, the dialogue indicates, applies to other disenfranchised segments of society, to the poor, and the black, as well as to women. Although the situations of the three groups parallel each other in important ways, and although, as a Quaker, Brown had, no doubt, strong feelings against slavery, the focus of this particular work is on women exclusively. The claim that he has Mrs. Carter make, that a member of a particular oppressed group can best speak for the rights of that group, is one which finds assent today. Brown, who was a member of none of these classes raised a voice against inequity by imagining a woman who could speak for herself. The limits of her range are perhaps the price paid for her power.

Yet women who, refusing to be barnyard animals, try to retain their human identity are seemingly trapped, whichever way they turn. They can reject the implied assessment of the politicians and refuse to "smile at . . . tyranny, or receive, as . . . gospel a code based on such atrocious maxims" as those which imply that women exist solely for the convenience and comfort of men. But this rejection seems to necessitate a withdrawal into a private realm which the discussions in Parts I and II reveal as but a mirror of the public one. A social system which, insofar as it respects women at all, respects most those who are, or have been, married, and which acts on the belief that husband and wife are one, and that one the husband, can hardly be said to offer women any viable alternative to their public nullity. The relations among politics, society, and sex are functional not causal; oppression in one sphere necessitates oppression in all.

Alcuin is finally driven to admit that prejudice, not reason, controls his attitude towards women, but reason, as we know all too well, is not sufficient to dispel a convenient belief. Thus Alcuin is not threatened by female wit or misery because he can regard them as exceptional. He can dismiss Mrs. Carter's demands for the perquisites and privileges of men by saying that these are not worth gaining, particularly not at the price that would inevitably have to be paid. What he wants—and he is someone, it should be remembered, who is sympathetic to women—is not a female senator or president, but a "household deity"! If the wish can no longer be justified, it can still persist, particularly when power supports attitudes and makes action of belief.

The second half of the dialogue, Parts III and IV, suggest routes out of this dead end through acts of imagination and redefinition. In his tale of the paradise of women, Alcuin constructs an imaginary civilization peopled by beings whose lives are governed by the rules that Mrs. Carter had suggested. Men and women are considered equally reasonable, equally valuable. All work necessary to secure food, clothing, and shelter is evenly distributed between the sexes on the grounds that sharing makes all work less onerous and that if neither sex has reason to envy the other both will be happier. When the necessary work is done all are equally free to act as their wishes and their talents dictate. There are no arbitrary restrictions on education, conversation, employment, or even dress—a freedom that perhaps loomed larger in previous centuries than it does today. Although, or perhaps because, the paradise of women is palpably fictive, is a place reached by mental rather than physical travel, it validates Mrs. Carter's arguments in a way that logic by itself could not. Alcuin is made radical even before he is bested in his arguments with the paradisal citizen, since that being is a creature of his own creation. The function of utopias is not so much to provide exact models but to jog the mind into channels of perception which are permanently blocked by its ordinary procedures.

Surprisingly, however, when Alcuin suggests that marriage, which Mrs. Carter had described as merely society's way of licensing the personal oppression of women, does not exist in his new society, she balks. She can imagine a large part of the system that Alcuin has been describing. Indeed, it is largely her invention; Alcuin has merely provided a structural framework and some connectives. But, her imagination is tied to the continuing existence of two givens: a vocabulary and a pattern. Mrs. Carter's proposed reforms are premised on the actualization of existing political promises and on the extension to women of those rights and obligations which men take for granted. The model is there. Mrs. Carter wants it doubled more than changed. A society in which the word marriage does not exist, however, is dangerous because, to Mrs. Carter, the removal of the word leaves a vacuum. Other words—libertinism, sensuality—and the patterns established by them will rush in to fill the void. Mrs. Carter would keep the term but change the customs, abridging some masculine freedoms and augmenting some feminine privileges. Fidelity would be obligatory for both sexes. Women would have property rights and private lives, as men do. To facilitate privacy and minimize boredom, married couples could live apart, seeing each other only as both wished. The grounds for divorce should be extended and women should be allowed to initiate proceedings. Interestingly, the emphasis on friendship and mutuality which appears in Mrs. Carter's concluding definition of marriage turns up with increasing frequency in writings by nineteenth and twentieth-century women authors. The dream of married friends is the dream of marriage between equals. It cannot be actualized unless the other arrangements for equality are made.

Alcuin is a document of obvious contemporary significance. The problems it raises are still with us and the voice which raises them is still our voice. Just as it would be absurd to deny that progress has been made since Mrs. Carter stood amidst the teacups and railed against her political and social exclusion, so it would be absurd to assert that the millenium is upon us. Because men and women still, too often, regard each other as ornaments and machines and still engage in parallel rather than shared activities, they are still, too often, limited and unequal beings. The trails Brown blazed are still not super highways, but remain footpaths, tangled and overgrown, though perhaps less so than when Brown first opened them. As we walk along them we need still be watchful and, of necessity, a little lonely.

This facsimile of The Gehenna Press
edition of Alcuin: A Dialogue
was printed for Grossman Publishers
by Noble Offset Printers, New York.
The type is Centaur & Arrighi.
The pressman for the original edition
was Harold McGrath. The text was
designed by Leonard Baskin.